7

TOUCH WOOD

TOUCH WOOD

SHORT STORIES

JOE ASHBY PORTER

TURTLE POINT PRESS

NEW YORK

"A Man Wanted to Buy a Cat" and "Scrupulous Amédée"
appeared in *The Kenyon Review*; "Naufrage and Diapason"
appeared in *Fiction* and was reprinted in *Voices from Home:
The North Carolina Prose Anthology*; "Bone Key" and "Icehouse
Burgess" appeared in *The Yale Review*; "An Errand" appeared
in *Fiction International*; "In the Mind," © The North Carolina
Museum of Art, appeared in *The Store of Joys: Writers Celebrate
the North Carolina Museum of Art's 50th Anniversary*; and
"Touch Wood" appeared in *The Carolina Quarterly*.

LCCN 2002103859   ISBN 1-885586-64-7

Design and composition by Jeff Clark
at Wilsted & Taylor Publishing Services

FOR YVES

CONTENTS

▼

The man wanted to buy the cat but couldn't because his wife was allergic to it. The allergy produced sneezing fits and watery eyes, and worsened at each exposure. Neither Chicklet daughter suffered from the malady, nor did the stringbean son. The youngsters, more or less sharing Popsy's wish, and excoriating Momsy behind her back, hatched a plot to post announcements at the supermarket, at the quiet ski lifts for early snowbirds, and under the bridge to give tramps a fair chance, announcements of an unspecified prize for the development of a super-loud cat bell together with comfortable sound-damping cat earplugs, but no contestant applied.

The cat would have washed its brindled face contentedly in the bustling family room or on the wife's pillow, or in the window of the man's woodworking and ski repair shop, as it did across the street in the window of its owner's millinery shop, where it had lived since it was a foundling kitten brought there years before by the milliner, herself already wizened then, whose turtle had expired and who, nocturnally scavenging for inspiration down back streets under a harvest moon, had heard a mewing at her heels. It continued around a corner, along an alleyway, around another corner, so piteously that the milliner stopped and peered back at the little beast.

Eventually she dropped it by the scruff of its neck into her workbasket and shut the cover. An hour later she let herself into her shop, set the basket on the worktable as was her wont, locked up, and climbed the spiral stair at the back of the shop to her living quarters. She was sitting on her spindle bed combing lint out of her hair when a faint mewing reminded her of the kitten. She donned a nightie and slippers and returned to the shop with a dish of warmed milk. The kitten lapped as the milliner improvised a litter box. Thus the kitten took up residence among wooden blocking heads. As the milliner worked, it toyed with ribbons and thimbles. Before it reached maturity the milliner had it declawed, to spare her livelihood.

The cat's mind tracked seamlessly across present variables, noting changes to the most minuscule, fleeting, and intangible—atmospheric pressure, magnetism—and effortlessly screening out all that settled into predictability, with scarcely a trace of self-consciousness, yet with a certain hovering retentiveness. It almost knew its name. Down the years, sometimes of an evening in the shuttered lamplight of the worktable, the milliner absorbed in a new confection, the cat gazed at the bright, lined face, pins protruding from the whiskered mouth, with something approaching recognition, as ancient laughter subsided, surfacing in the white static of the pictureless television the milliner used for a radio.

The man had grown up in a spacious high-rise apartment decorated with photographs of dairy cattle, and next door had lived a retired cardiologist and her sagging bulldog. At eastern schools, at the last of which the man and his wife met and fell in love, more

than one acquaintance had had an animal companion, spaniels, a lame rhesus. The man associated these
details the Wednesday when, the ski season winding
down, he closed up shop early and stepped across the
street to help his wife select an Easter bonnet, and first
noticed the cat. On a needlepoint footstool it stretched
and yawned. Scarcely had the man entered the shop,
behind his wife, who went directly to the display window to consider a raspberry straw boater, when the cat
trotted across to him and curvetted between his ankles
as though he were a friend of yore. Thenceforth into
the summer the man found excuses—the mayoral
election, the billboard issue—to visit the milliner's
cat. By July he had discovered in himself a need to own
this cat.

His wife, knowing her disability, had taken the pre-
caution of airing her bonnet behind the chalet a good
twenty-four hours, and even so had found it necessary
during the Easter morning service to stifle one sneeze
and to release another in the guise of a hallelujah, and
to dab her eyes as if in response to the minister's elo-
quence, so that there could be no question of her co-
habiting with the cat, as the man well knew, but he
thought it might live in the playhouse, a scaled-down

version of the chalet that the triplets had outgrown, assuming the milliner would be willing to part with it, or else his wife might agree to undertake the costly and time-consuming series of tests that might—no way of knowing before the fact—produce a serum for her allergy.

She declined the latter solution but agreed at least to entertain the former, albeit with misgivings, for even assuming he could shower and change after each visit to the cat house—he envisioned installing an adult shower at the back, supplied with water from the buried sprinkler system, heated in a water heater installed under an eave against the shower, which could drain over the gneiss down the mountainside—and he envisioned using environmentally friendly space-age soap—and the same plumbing could serve the laundry he envisioned installing next to the shower, so that he himself could tend to his contaminated vestments—even so, she thought, and even with any number of other shifts, still she would have to live with the real possibility of waking in the middle of some dark night unable to breathe.

She told the children, "I wouldn't give it a moment's consideration if I didn't love him up one side and down the other. One day you'll understand, if you're lucky. It won't necessarily be spouse number one, or any spouse for that matter, and given your age (eight) I wouldn't want to lay money on what gender or race it might be, for instance, but trust me, you'll know how lucky you're fortunate enough to be if it does eventually happen to you. Who knows, you could conceivably stumble on a foretaste next week even. Stranger things have happened."

"Cut to the chase, Ma."

"As I was on the verge of saying, it has to be love, otherwise I'd deliver an ultimatum, it or me. If he turned out to have his priorities upside-down, your Denver auntie would be happy for me to move in with them. For that matter, I've kept myself up and this isn't 12th-century India. The manicurist always says he's never seen such beautiful nails."

"Give us a break, Ma."

"Tell you what: I will go so far as to inquire as to whether shaving the cat might do the trick. I have a feeling the hair's at least the vector, and maybe the causative agent. And after all, hairless cats exist, I've seen pictures of them grooming the imaginary pelt, or coat."

"You betcha, Ma." They nickered after she left the room.

As the man steamed, bent, glued, and clamped laminate, as he turned spindles, as he leafed through *Snowboarding*, he mulled over strategy. The main question, as he saw it, was axiological. While he felt willing to pay the milliner many times the cat's objective worth, assuming that could be determined, he well knew that people sometimes called pets priceless. Furthermore he had an uneasy suspicion that courts somewhere or other—something he had read in a law review at the dentist's?—had at least entertained the possibility. Thumping a watermelon at the greengrocer's, he reminded himself of infungibility: probably the milliner would balk at replacing her cat with another, however similar, even a clone whose maturation could somehow be accelerated, if that was a requirement. When push came to shove she would probably prove no readier than, come to think of it, he, to be satisfied with another cat. For that matter, an alternate cat would likely provoke similar reactions in his wife. Then there was the problem of game psychology. Even supposing (what was anything but evident) some threshold such that the milliner would be unable to refuse any offer above it, it might be extravagant, for probably there was a much lower range of sums she could refuse but wouldn't. Call these two ranges D (the higher) and B. Below B of course lay A, sums so low she would certainly refuse them. He could discount them but not the more problematic range C, of sums low enough to refuse, and which she would refuse because they seemed insultingly high. The ideal offer would be in the B range, high there, yet not so high as to risk straying into C and putting the royal kibosh on the whole undertaking. He sighed and doodled with a forefinger in the turnings on his worktable. After all, before talking figures it might be prudent to feel her out about the possibility. He glanced at the cuckoo clock: ten AM, as good a time as any in a July Wednesday to hang up his leather apron, close shop, and amble across the cobbled street for a chat.

In the milliner's display window, opaque paper domes still protected her confections from the morning sun. There among them, attracted by the warmth and perhaps also, the man thought, by the look of what might seem a dozen covered birdcages, snoozed the cat. The jingle of the doorbell waked it, and it came to sharpen imaginary claws on the man's gabardine pant leg as he sat on the fitting stool before the milliner. She pinned a clump of russet cobweb to a dusty pink felt toque. "Send your Ms. by for a gander at this number," she said. "In my apprenticehood folks said redheads oughtn't wear pink, but nowadays it's the exact reverse."

"Mmm," said the man.

"How long have you two been married, incidentally? Unless I'm assuming too much, and you're one of these newer couples that turn their nose up at matrimony."

"No, I wouldn't say we turn our 'nose' up at much of anything, really. Seventeen years solid next month."

"Hats off to you."

The man shrugged. "I know what you mean, and thanks, but the truth of the matter is, we never seemed to have a choice."

"I suppose you dated other carrottops first." She laid a medallion of crushed auburn velvet against the brim, considering.

The man tugged an ear and smiled. "I generally think of carrottops as green. But no, and not any other color either. It was love at first sight, freshman year.

Before, at a unisex prep school, coed now of course, and so much the better, I did escort the odd young lady to a prom or flick, but not anybody repeatedly enough to call it dating." He pulled the ear once more. "You probably won't believe this, but I lost my virginity with my wife-to-be. Did you ever ski yourself?"

The milliner sniffed. "Do I look as if I ever skied?"

"It's not too late, you know. I see women older than you on the slopes. Men too." He scratched the cat's back. "The fresh air does wonders, and the beginner slopes couldn't be milder."

"I do believe you're trying to make a sale." She replaced the medallion with a sprig of mock parsley.

"I could give you a deal, for sure. Make you the envy of the mountain. I think we ought to scratch each other's backs. Hell, I'd be happy to make you a gift of a pair, it would give me such pleasure to see you out on the subtoboggan run in powder, against the frisky conifers. I suppose you'd want to design your own ski bonnet, but as for . . ."

"My niece skis."

"Well then, maybe she . . ."

"Nephew too."

"Ah. You don't say."

"Both nephews, now I remember, the grandniece as well. Papa too, and both brothers did. You might think I had it in the blood, but I never was athletic. I'm legally blind in one eye, so I lack depth perception." She sewed on the sprig at a Tyrolean angle. With a spot of superglue she affixed a triangle of iridescent vinyl nearby—not so near the sprig as to make one figure, yet near enough to invite mutual reference. "But your wife, was she equally inexperienced before that frosh lightning bolt? I assume you and she had similar upbringings. Your school admitted only boys then, but it's easy to imagine a finishing school for her in the same region."

"Actually, no."

"Sorry?"

"She grew up in Budapest and Maryland, me in Minneapolis, and the upbringings differed quite a bit. Me an only and late child of dairy farmers, she next-to-youngest of four products of a bohemian life in the lower ranks of the diplomatic corps. No surprise then that she'd had two or three premarital flings." The cat groomed his wrist with its tiny rough tongue down into the palm, along the destiny line still welted from carpal tunnel surgery. "But don't worry, that's never been a problem. Love irons out lots of wrinkles." He picked the cat up. He felt its ribs under the sliding furred skin, like a delicate cage for a birdlike heart. "It conquers all, I might almost say."

The milliner shook her head. "I can't buy that, Buster. The world's too big. Present-day India alone, not to mention her larger neighbor to the northeast. Did poverty and illness slip your mind? Oh please, let's not babble. Conquest? In my experience love knuckles under to just about anything."

The man let the cat wriggle free. "To money?"

The milliner set aside her creation. "Well, I'm not exactly sure what you have in mind." She patted her lap. "Here, puss-puss." As if by telekinesis the cat translated itself there, where it curled and purred. "In any case love (whatever we mean by that) gets bowled over by desire. Not to mention need. Not even in the same league, really."

The man thought, if she refuses, I could catnap it early one Wednesday afternoon while she's dozing. Leave a bogus ransom note? No, why take needless risks? Cats wander off all the time, it's in their nature. They lack canine loyalty and stick-to-itiveness. Under lock and key, under wraps during this milliner's remaining years, my family sworn to secrecy, in the playhouse it and I could spin out its remaining days like birds in a gilded cage. I could learn to meow. He felt a catch in his throat.

The milliner leaned forward. Motes meandered in a swath of sunlight. Between thumb and forefinger she pressed imaginary claws out of their sheaths. "This one would leave its signature if it could, on my cha-peaux, on your leg." She laughed inaudibly.

The man thought, but what sort of example would that set for my family? The stringbean means to be a banker, a good one I feel sure, but with a background of concealing a purloined feline, one Friday at closing time in the vault, wouldn't he be tempted to pocket a wad? Wouldn't the Chicklets stray too? And who knows, the milliner might run mad with grief, after all. He nodded. "Did you ever have another pet?"

"Insects as a child, arachnids, segmented worms. Then zilch until some summers ago I was down in the valley trout fishing—I tie my own flies—and I opened my creel and what do you think?"

The man pictured a buzzing tray of bluebottles in bondage. "Not a clue."

"A turtle had somehow crawled in, and didn't want

to crawl out until we came home. I gave it the run of the place. At supper I leave the back door open and it could have taken a powder but it never did. Maybe it preferred the cat food I gave it, to acorns or whatever it could forage in the wild. Inside though it disappeared for weeks on end, sleeping or hibernating behind a broom. Then I found it in the pantry, all closed like when it slept, but when I set food before it nothing happened. After a week of that, I borrowed a stethoscope to check for breath or a heartbeat. It was in the spring, so I set it on the back stoop just in case. Through that summer and fall when I happened to notice it I'd pick it up and shake it. It seemed to get lighter. The next summer the shell blistered." She shook her head, clucking. "It had to croak for me to miss its company. So when this abandoned kitty-cat adopted me, I was ready."

As the man told his wife that evening, at this point his heart sank. Even buying the cat now seemed quite out of the question, even supposing the milliner could be persuaded to sell, it so evidently belonged with her. The man's heart sank and he seemed to feel his hair thinning. "Stiff upper, though?" he told himself in the ensuing months, "it's not the end of the world, for heaven's sake. And time heals.'' And yet as months lengthened a certain bleakness refused to lift, not even after his wife bought him a Chia pig for his workshop. He gave it good light and watered it dutifully, and as the terra cotta flanks sprouted, they sometimes brought a wan smile to his lips in the vestibule where he stamped the February snow from his boots, the March and April snow. Once he went so far as to give the foliage a light tousle.

For the sake of his family and friends and customers the man did his best to maintain a cheerful demeanor. Yet his wife knew that stronger measures were needed. Thus on Easter morning, the triplets gathered to witness, she presented her beloved husband with a baby bunny rabbit. It buoyed his spirits immediately.

Black and white like his parents' dairy cattle, it grew quickly to the size of a cat, and well beyond. It keeps the man company during his workdays, leaving clean odorless little turds about the shop, munching lettuces. He enjoys its hopping, on floors or grass or snow, and he especially enjoys its long moments of reflection as it watches him, not moving an ear, not a whisker. Life seems good. The triplets attend Ivies of their choice, one hardheaded daughter majors in lapidary science, the other, with an eye to membership in the first human Martian settlement, in agronomy, and Stringbean, an ace pole-vaulter, in economics. The man counts himself lucky above all in a wife to thank for these blessings. True love, man-to-man he tells the stringbean, is money in a bank.

NAUFRAGE AND DIAPASON

▼

Johnny John Hawk fingers aside the pitiful thin curtain his ex ran up from a patchy dishtowel. Johnny stretches his big head into the niche at the end of his bunk. Through a plexiglass window scarred as if it has been to the moon and back, and not much bigger than a spaghetti box, Johnny can see what the begrudging cold purple means dawning over the new snow and totem poles, and the bay where his Lorna bobs at anchor like a red toy. Trouble is what that sky means. Bad squalls and worse.

Snuggle back into the sleeping bag and hibernate a

week more? In these Alaskan waters this early in the spring it's only fifty-fifty you'll even locate salmon. Plus nephew Elmo perking coffee at the other end of the trailer is too green for weather like this, ought to be back at Ketchikan Middle School learning a trade, not hanging with a hand-to-mouth trawler uncle pushing forty squatting here on this lost bay. Elders say the cove had honor once. Now, with remains of a fishing camp that never got built, it looks like a frozen trainwreck on a landfill. Plus a hangover aching from one temple to the other like Frankenstein rods.

Plus. . . . But Johnny shakes his head and lets the curtain spread back into place. He unzips his mummy bag and rolls out of the bunk. The sockeye should be running. Except . . . what was it a moment ago in the sky, a shade north of the tall totem, wheeling behind a precipice of cloud, an eagle?

When Elmo hears Johnny slump to the john and pee, he films a black skillet with bear grease and cracks in six eggs. By the time he has shaken out and divided an omelette filled with roe, meanwhile toasting bread over the second gas ring in a vintage four-sided holder with hinged sloping sides, Uncle Johnny himself has taken his place at the eating table, and is praying the way he does before he eats anything or even tastes the BC fizzing in his toothbrush glass. Elmo sets the food and coffee on the table.

Elmo's mother, Johnny's ex's younger sister, told Elmo he could lay out of school two weeks in May here, on two conditions. One is, apply himself when he gets back, which means more study, less firewater, condoms. Elmo expects to finesse that condition, but he's not so sure about the other, which is, talk to Johnny about maybe coming to Ketchikan and getting on welfare, maybe signing on as night watchman at the cannery or custodian at the high school. Last night near midnight when they stumbled out to view the auroras, Elmo had almost broached the subject. Maybe today? Or maybe never. The dude's life is shot, so how much good could leaning on a broom handle do? Still, maybe today all the same. There's television in Ketchikan, monthly social dancing.

Johnny sometimes prays to the Great Spirit or the Blessed Virgin but now he's studying how to say no if Elmo asks for money or some other kind of help. Maybe Elmo could handle the truth that Uncle Johnny's at the end of his rope. Cash for Lorna payments and alimony ran out in October, and cash for hooch and groceries won't last through May. Johnny's been squatting and living off the land, but any day now the marshal will show up with repo papers and maybe a warrant.

Johnny looks up and unfolds his hands. Ice cracks and thunks into snow outside. Johnny tells Elmo he'll take the Lorna out alone today for a shakedown trawl through a near passage, and be back before dark. He asks Elmo to fill a thermos.

Okay, says Elmo. But you know I was thinking. Us Tlingits, we ought to open us up a casino and kick back, forget salmon.

Lest I forget my love for thee, sings Johnny.

Down at the pier icy froth scumbles around pilings and against the wooden dory. Casting off, Johnny takes Elmo's hand and says, stroke the thunderbird pole with that same hand for me on your way back up to the trailer. Me, I forgot.

Check, but it doesn't seem like you, Johnny. We must've partied you too hard last night. So look lively out there.

No, says Johnny as he pushes off with an oar. Truth is, I stopped myself from touching that pole. My hand went out automatically but then some devil got into me and I said fuck it. But now I'm having second thoughts. You carry the touch back up and it should be the same.

Don't worry, says Elmo. When he reaches the pole he pushes his open hand hard against the frozen wood, back and forth until down on the water Johnny has anchored and boarded the Lorna and turned to wave, and Elmo can wave back with his other hand.

Through the day Elmo listens to short wave, and writes half a letter to his girlfriend, and naps, and listens to the radio some more. Going on three he loses the signal in spumes of interference. A little later a deep whistle sounds from the harbor, from a strange boat. Ahoy, ahoy, rattles the ship-to-shore set. It's a fisherman from Wrangell come to tell Elmo his mother's in the hospital with a burst gall bladder. Elmo leaves Johnny a note under the salt shaker and locks up, more against bears than people. At the helm, the captain with walrus moustaches says the hospital transmitter bounced word off a satellite, an operation scheduled for twenty minutes ago. Good odds, the surgeon's supposed to have said. Maybe on the way out to a clear channel they'll glimpse Johnny heading in. Dusk, a ribbed sky, frozen ribbed water with black umbrellas opening in it, squalls.

Zrr, zrr. The twenty-three-year-old white woman with lank reddish hair, granny glasses, and braces, whose name is Frieda Wakeland, slides piecework left, right, out, and back. I never got asked to a sock hop, Frieda told Maudie Roberts, who shares her piecing table, so I guess that's why I hop these treadles in my sock feet. How 'bout yourself? Maudie said she'd got asked to an ice cream supper in the churchyard, the night dead Bobby popped the question and she accepted, but sock hops were more in her children's time and maybe the grandchildren's. At work Maudie's always preferred tartan fleece-lined house slippers for her bunions, or maybe it was a hammer toe she mentioned last week at lunch.

Frieda's worked in the riverfront Carolina hosiery mill since she was nineteen. Her pa, an upstanding Crittenden deacon and lay minister, had aimed for her to enroll for a church-related nursing degree out in southern Indiana, either that or learn tap for real at the Crittenden Academy of Dance behind the drygoods

store, so she could bring home more than the miniature plastic trophies lined up on her dresser, maybe a
contract from one of the televangelists she could send
a videotape audition to. When Frieda couldn't see her
way clear to go along with either plan, Pa sent her
down the street to let her rethink priorities working
minimum wage in the hosiery mill, no benefits, with
seven other local women, mothers and grandmoth-
ers, widows.

At the time, Frieda hadn't wanted to go off to nursing or television because she didn't want to leave Crittenden. Not that she cared much for the country back-
water near nothing except the impassable river that
provided nothing except alewives each spring and
power for the mill. Frieda hated Crittenden, really.
What had kept her there at first was love, at least that's
what she called it, for Eddie Thorne, six years her senior. He'd tried to scrape a living with sugar beets on
the farm he inherited from the auntie that raised him,
south on the county road, beets then tobacco and then
boo that landed him in the pen where he went bad and
stopped even writing, and then so had Frieda. Eddie'd
always worn rubbers, and the subject of marriage had
never come up, so that was okay.

Like meringue on the baked Alaska Maudie turned

out of her cast-iron stove a hundred years ago to snag her dead Bobby with, fabric ripples and billows sliding to the sewing foot, each blend wrinkling in its own way, rayon-polyester, rayon-cotton-polyester, each with its own name, Lureen, Softex, Lureen Twill. Once, Frieda goes, which is your favorite? Maudie goes, blends pshaw, before you was born, sugar, we used to sew pure goods, even linen.

Is an interloper a kind of deer, Frieda remembers asking Pa, after grace at breakfast. She was nine and Ma had only been gone a year. A schoolmate's mother had explained that since Ma was an interloper, you could see how she might prance back out of Critten-den one fine day, as she did. Pa hasn't remarried. He keeps busy lettering and sign-painting, and with his ham radio and of course the church, and his health seems to be holding for the moment. Says he doesn't know Ma's whereabouts or desire to.

Muzzle up for the race, cracked Frieda this morning before the whistle, because of the Bakelite breath filter masks the crew wears to protect against textile dust, and she was recalling a science show about dog races. Greyhounds muzzled but not huskies in the Iditarod (not Izod), the opposite of what you'd expect, really.

Frieda wears earplugs too, against the noise. You learn to read lips. While Frieda sews she runs stories in her mind, that unfold and settle like cloth.

Pa is lettering a blue roadsign for the Herring Shack down river when over his ham set comes a bulletin, escaped convicts camped in the wildwood. Planning to blast their way into Crittenden, two whites and a half-breed, beating drums and singing. One of the whites rumored to be lovelorn for a Crittenden spitfire who spurns him. Pa swishes his lettering brush in thinner and shakes dry the bristles. Moments later in the den he secretes his wedding ring and billfold behind a trick board. Now he kneels, humming the doxology.

Zrr, zrr. The livid sun seems to hang motionless in the freezing heavens as the tormented western horizon rises to it. Loaded with sockeye and some coho, the Lorna trundles through a high chop and wind stiffening to gale force.

Overdue caulking, the Lorna seems to have sprung a leak. In the hold the salmon are swimming again, bumping each other in the dark, trailing tackle like Mail Pouch from their cruel underslung mouths. Above at the wheel, Johnny estimates he will have time to spare. The cannery should buy most of the catch, and Johnny thinks, why not ship a nice fish to the new President's little girl, for her salmon hair. Maybe one for Arthur Godfrey and all the Little Godfreys too, that Johnny's ex-mother-in-law used to like on Ketchikan radio. Something in the engine or the drive sputters. Johnny gears down and flips on the ship-to-shore.

Frieda snips the thread. She pushes the nightie over the edge onto a conveyor belt that will move it past finishing and inspection. As she taps the counting machine she checks her liquid crystal wristwatch for the first time since lunch. As she hooks up the next batch of piecework out of the tumbrel beside her folding chair she steals her first glance since lunch at the fly-specked skylight. Were she Alice with the giraffe neck she might nudge it open and peer around in the foolish sunshine, while her hands stayed busy.

The ship-to-shore fails to respond. Johnny tries again. No dice, dead catheters or something. The Lorna is sideslipping and yawing. Johnny keys a different map onto his screen and plots a different course, to the nearest docking. He shifts back into full forward. The engine hums as if considering. Then it retches and gives up the ghost. Through his legs Johnny feels a shudder as the Lorna begins to founder.

Johnny thinks what it will be like to go down in these icily sloshing dark waves of ocean sea, with a life unspooling before his eyes. Water will fill his lungs. He'll empty them, and fill them again with water.

Two days later at lunch hour Elmo gets through to a maritime warden who's swung by Johnny's cove and seen nor hide nor hair of him. Thoughtfully chewing a stick of pemmican, Elmo saunters back to the bleachers. He has a funny feeling, he tells his girlfriend. He says the same thing that evening to his ma and her boyfriend at the kitchen table over red flannel hash. When his ma calls her sister for her birthday the second week of June she says, thanks for the carnations when they did my gall bladder, Lorna. By the way, looks like your Johnny's shipped out for parts unknown, but I know you already gave up hope for alimony checks.

Months pass and years. Elmo moves to Nome. Once at his mailbox he thinks maybe he'll find a picture postcard from Johnny. After a while Elmo forgets his uncle. He sells Toyotas, opens his own dealership in Yessum, marries, raises two children, dies during an earthquake. His aquamarine class ring gleaming in the rubble leads investigators to the body. Tough luck, says the captain, dusting off her viscose coveralls. The lieutenant shrugs, snaps open her gas mask, and says he had a rich full life probably. One of Elmo's children assumes the dealership.

Maudie reaches across the table and taps Frieda with a yardstick. When Frieda pulls out an earplug Maudie says, my Junie needs a sitter Monday week if your neighbor's girl wants pin money. Alaska, chirps Frieda. She stuffs the plug back in. Zrr, zrr. The pieced yoke she slides off the table billows like a liquid map.

A widowed society dentist planning to summer in Crittenden seeks a hygienist trainee between twenty and twenty-five years of age. Running the tip of her tongue against her braces, Frieda tastes waterpack salmon, an impulse purchase from the Piggly Wiggly. Frieda wanted to be able to say she'd tried it at least once in her life.

Now the prison escapees have Pa hostage and they're barricading themselves. Helicopters buzz in from Charlotte, and armed hovercraft ascend the river. In a skirmish the desperadoes are recaptured. Unharmed, Pa testifies in their behalf on national television, before the sheriff herds all three into his paddy wagon and whisks them back for more decades in the slammer.

What is a life after all but a piece of stretched meat? The story ratchets along regardless. In a sci-fi Frieda rented last Sunday for her birthday, this gob will settle on your face and you can't pry it off, any more than you can pry off the world. That's right, Frieda thinks. Zrr, zrr. People find themselves at dead ends all the time, up a creek. Pa and Frieda have widescreen in the den, hordes succumb daily. So what else is new? And yet. . . .

Johnny has swum out the pilothouse and risen toward the dim choppy surface, almost free, until a part of the superstructure has caught his ankle, and it is too late now to struggle. Johnny goes feet first into the green black. His arms trail above his upturned face, his poor fingers already frozen. The Lorna's hull collapses. One by one, sockeye and coho nose through the rupture out into the depths and away toward western rivers.

SCHREKX AND SON

▼

Alain Schrekx lived with his son Gerald in a basement apartment off the Rue Pezous in Toulon, France. Every morning Alain woke at six in time to give his full set of real teeth a good scrub before preparing café au lait for himself and Gerald, who had to be at work at eight-thirty downtown in the Palace of Justice, answering telephone questions and daydreaming. Having waved his son off, Alain busied himself about a routine that varied little day in day out, rain, shine.

Weekdays, after perusing horses' names in the *Var Matin*, and performing a calculation based on his horoscope, he swished the coffee bowls in a pail of cloudy water, strewed corn on a feeder for a magpie, and walked to the nearest tobacconist, where he placed bets in the amount of twenty francs and bought a daily ration of as many cigarettes. Then he might take a bus to see a doctor, an accountant, or an official concerned with one of his retirement accounts—a pension from his years delivering mail in a Toulon suburb, a small income purchased before Gerald's birth with winnings from a good numbers morning, and income from Eulalie's life insurance—or go to the open market at the Pont du Las for produce, or to the Arab butcher there for merguez, or to the fishmonger for a delectable morsel, and to the wine merchant and the baker. "How's it going today, Alain?" a merchant might ask, or a waiter at the bar where he took a midmorning coffee. Alain would smile, shake his head, sniffle, and say, "Not bad, my friend. Could be worse."

Noon found Alain back at the apartment. Weather permitting he lunched barefoot at the orange metal table in his courtyard, and distributed scraps on the bird feeder. When greed overcame a clumsy magpie and it clambered out of the air onto the far edge, Alain crooked a finger and clucked in a way that once had persuaded a sparrow to hop aboard, but the magpie merely looked askance and scolded, ratta-tat-tatta-tat. In summer a ratcheting cicada made a trio with Alain and the bird.

Before leaving the table Alain tried astral projection. He aimed to leave his earthly body motionless in the chair and perch his astral body on a neighbor's window ledge, or at least atop the courtyard wall. He had learned of the procedure from a Radio Monte Carlo call-in program. Once or twice he had felt himself on the verge of success, as with the Keno results he then went in through the beaded curtain to learn of on television. With them, and with the Loto, over the years Alain kept a running tally and, while he knew that his balance showed a mild steady decline overall, still a big win could always happen.

Early afternoons Alain spent in his bedroom, napping or playing "Nights in White Satin" on his synthesizer. In mid-afternoon he locked up again and bussed down to the Leon Blum Foyer des Anciens, a concrete meeting room with six chairs, on a scrap of terrain squeezed into a triangle against the wall of St. Roch prison. Alone in the gravel courtyard there he sat on the immovable nickel-plated steel mesh bench under the olive tree for two or three hours, hands folded in his lap. No pie perched in this olive tree, nor any other bird, nor even any cicada through the dry summers, but now and again a lizard snaked down the stucco wall of the prison onto the municipal refuse cannister, and stood on its toes to watch Alain, and bob its head as if signaling.

For years the prison had been scheduled for demolition, but no firm date had been set, and the 18th-century pile still functioned. Walking to and from the Anciens, Alain Schrekx sometimes came in sight of a prisoner at a high cell window. No prison window overlooked the courtyard, for beyond the high common wall topped with razor wire lay the prison yard. Sometimes over the wall came the bark of a guard, prisoners' grunts and cries of "Ouf! Ouf!," thuds of shoulders and backs against gravel, as the inmates played an abbreviated rugby under the direction of a retired Toulonais coach, so that they might learn better to control aggressive impulses. Here again Alain might attempt bodily displacement. Once he managed so to concentrate that inside his leather sandals, in each pearl-grey anklet each toe curled separately, as if

Alain were picking out "Nights in White Satin" with his feet.

Soon after five-thirty each evening, barring accident, Alain left the Anciens and walked to the Palace of Justice, which adjoined the prison on its opposite side, where under the rippling tricolor and the chiseled *Liberté Egalité Fraternité* he met Gerald leaving work. Together they bussed home. Gerald prepared supper and his brown bag lunch for the next day. Wednesdays at seven-thirty they watched the transparent blue plastic Loto drum deposit one by one seven dancing colored numbered plastic spheres in line for the day's winners and losers. Every weeknight they watched television, news as they dined and then a light movie.

The little household spent weekends on chores and television game shows, and each Saturday evening at seven-thirty they again watched the Loto spheres tumble into place. On the third Friday of the month they dined at a cafeteria downtown. Each chose one of the day's specials, and each began with his own preferred first course, rollmops or muzzle salad for Alain, charcuterie or boar paté for Gerald. They spent half of Gerald's annual vacation quietly at home, and for the remaining two weeks they rented a tent at a campground conveniently located off the Toulon-Marseille autoroute.

Last year they chose the second two weeks of September for camping, when the off-season rate would leave aside a bit more for Alain to bet with. Theirs being the only tent in the sector, and with the shush of the autoroute traffic, the occasion invited intimate talk from sleeping bag to sleeping bag through the dusty evenings, especially when the mistral began to blow at the beginning of the second week. At length Gerald broached a subject that had been on his mind. "Papa, of course I learned about procreation in school, and like everybody else I've seen my share of movie love scenes, and I have heard my share of jokes."

Alain chuckled indulgently.

Gerald continued. "Still, I can't help wondering what it's really like, especially should she happen to be a virgin."

A moment passed. Alain moistened his lips. "A good question. It deserves a good answer, except. . . ." Another moment. Alain sucked his teeth. "What might have raised it just now?"

" 'What'?"

"As I said. It would be good to know."

Gerald stared at the tent roof. "Yes, Papa. In truth I hoped you would wonder just that. My question was a ploy, you see, for I have a confession to make. Or really a kind of announcement." Convicts, Gerald reminded his papa, were led from the Palace of Justice into St. Roch prison through a tunnel under the common wall. From his desk at the phone bank in the Palace basement Gerald over the years had watched any number of condemned men, a few of them acquaintances, and one or two celebrities, bid liberty goodbye at the entrance to the ill-famed tunnel. When the electronic plungers and pin-lights of the lock stirred, never had anyone but the bailiffs, or else a janitor, stepped from behind the heavy door when it swung open, before last St. John's day morning, when who should creep grinning into the flourescent anteroom but Miss Ida Guetaly, a dishwasher in the prison mess who had learned the day's code and tried it for a lark.

Alain cleared his throat and snuffled. "Not prudent of this Miss."

"Prudent?"

"She might have been missed on the other side. Although it would prove her honesty, I suppose."

"How, Papa?"

"Someone less scrupulous would have turned a tidy profit with her knowledge. But then maybe she already had, or has. Maybe prisoners have been vacating St. Roch via the tunnel nightly into the streets of Toulon."

"Unreported?"

"Possibly, to avert scandal. Stranger things have happened."

"No, Papa, no. The code changes daily. Ida had only chanced to learn that day's."

"Ah. You call each other by first names."

"Yes, in fact. She only dared peek out, you see, but it made me laugh. She laughed too, and we agreed to meet for lunch up in the Place d'Armes. We've lunched there twice, and once in the Justice canteen."

Alain shifted jerkily. "How old is this Ida?"

"Four years younger than I, twenty-seven next November. Mouse-like, you know? Pert but innocent, with short dun hair and black eyes. She knows more jokes than anyone I ever met. Her favorite color is pea-green and she loves to collect postage stamps. I told her that you used to carry mail."

"Toulonais parents, I suppose."

"More or less. Her father was a green card Arab who's returned to the Sahel. Her mother abandoned her to the state when she started school. I thought we might invite her to the cafeteria the next time."

"Hum, hum." Alain switched on the weak lantern, withdrew one leg from the bag, crooked it and began to work on his toenails, letting the clippings fall onto his stomach. "Your mama Eulalie was mousy too," he said. "And also a virgin. You were conceived on our wedding night."

"Wedding night," murmured Gerald. "Were you happy, Papa?"

"We can't learn everything from the movies and jokes. You asked about the first time. Well, Gerald, when you probe your tootie into a virgin, a real virgin, she makes a loud pop. Her maidenhead pops. And then . . ."

Gerald now interrupted, "Oh Papa. Oh dear, I didn't know."

"Many don't. It caught Eulalie herself by surprise. All she could think of to do, poor thing, was release a shame-faced snicker. Which did have at least one advantage."

Gerald twitched.

Alain continued, "It did cover some of the other sounds. Her hair spread on the pillow like spaghetti. Ah Eulalie, ah marriage. It wasn't a month before the phone calls started. Thank heavens you were spared knowing. Anonymous whispering, to the post office with aspersions about, oh, you can imagine. Three or four, only, that I ignored, and yet there they were." Alain withdrew his other leg to trim its toes. "I have wondered," he began, and then broke off. Outside a magpie scolded an arboreal rat.

"Have you ever heard of an episiotomy, Gerald?" Alain described the procedure, snip-snipping the air with his nail scissors. "Usually it suffices, but not with poor Eulalie."

After a moment Gerald said, "No?"

"No, because you were too pudgy. A C-section might have saved her, but it was too late by the time they considered that, with all the tearing and blood. She only lasted an hour, crying 'Shriek! Shriek!' Of course it wasn't your fault. I determined then and there not to remarry, but rather," Alain sucked his teeth, "to devote my life to you, in memory of your poor mother."

Gerald lay still. The variable mistral sounded like

surf, now a bigger wave, now smaller ones. If you listen long enough to surf you begin to be able to make some accurate predictions. Those who claim that big waves arrive at intervals of seven are not far wrong, for as you track their intervals you realize you might spend a lifetime on a beach without hearing fourteen little waves in succession, or two big ones. At the same time, it might also take a lifetime for forty-nine successive waves to obey the law, nor does any wave come labeled big or small.

Alain brushed his clippings onto the tent floor, and then swept them into a tidy heap, which he slid under his sleeping bag pillow. "Let's cogitate about the cafeteria. We may need to do some belt-tightening. Lately I've bet a fraction more in anticipation of your annual pay raise, but the numbers have frowned on us. Nighty-night."

In the ensuing weeks, what with one thing and another, relations cooled between Gerald and his friend Ida, and she has since married a sanitation worker. With a run of luck Alain recouped some losses, and could invest part of Gerald's next paycheck in a portable television set. On their next camping trip they will be able to know how Alain's bets have fared as soon as the numbers are announced, rather than having to wait until the next day's paper. A radio would have served for the daily noontime Keno numbers. Even for the semiweekly evening Loto numbers Alain could have heard the results on radio, but he needed television to watch the numbered spheres tumble. The transparent plastic drum seemed at once empty and compressed, as if the numbers were clicking and dancing in laughing gas. When Alain scratched his whiskers before the screen, he could almost feel his sinuses expand as the spheres hopped one by one onto their ledge to compose the day's sequence. In Alain's mind above the Loto theme swelled a paso doble synth "Nights in White Satin." He rubbed his nose, like a prestidigitator coaxing coins out a child's.

—Know why we made Ripley's column back in thirty-six? Ink sketch with hand lettering: Duval Street, Key West Florida, Runs from the Atlantic Ocean to the Gulf of Mexico. Plus, believe it or not, as you know (what did you say your name was?), the old Strand down the block has just reopened as a Ripley's Odditoreum.

These three nymphs, Alison whose hair I'm wrapping now, and her already wrapped pals, Katie and Barb, no, Babs, sorry, it was on the tip of my tongue (my ex-wife was Barb, but that's another story), these three Graces must have passed our grand old dame, whose eyeshadow the Ripley folks have merely freshened.

These damsels didn't venture out into the moral ambiguities of a tropical night alone. They've been here in Paradise since Monday, with Alison's parents, and tonight they stepped out with Alison's dad for a look at the street of dreams. When they saw me, each knew she had to wear a hair wrap back to Cleveland. Alison's dad pressed on, to check out the wet tee-shirt contest. Only kidding there, girls.

I charge the going rate, a dollar an inch, so as not to disadvantage other hair wrappers. Except for them I'd do it for free. I wrap for wrapping's sake, and for an excuse to be here. I work days for IBM up in Boca Raton. You wouldn't believe my salary and benefits, and my position wasn't even glanced at during the layoffs you may have read about. Once or twice a week after work I drive down here, arrive about eight, park, spread my rug, open my tray of floss and beads, light a stick of incense.

People are curious. Some pass and come back, like you, to find out what the story is. Singles, pairs too, families. The average wrap takes me twenty minutes, depending on how long the hair might happen to be, and the ornamentation. It's like a coaxial cable. The person picks colors and patterns. As you can see, I have the whole rainbow here in embroidery floss. On these bracelets I wear samples. Katie opted for classic half-inch bands, wine and fuchsia. Babs surprised me, she wanted taupe with only the occasional lavender ring. Alison's going with this inch fade between pink and orange. Give her a word of encouragement about how good it's looking.

The location can be anywhere on the scalp. Alison's, off-center at the back of the crown, is a classic choice, really. I separate the strands to be wrapped, and slip them through the slot in the cardboard square, a temporary guard to keep the lucky lock's neighbors out of the action. How about you when I get done with Alison? What did you say your name is? I'm Sky.

—Megga, but don't start, I've already heard it and anyway it's with two g's. I did have one of those deals once upon a time, before these three were born. But that was then. Nothing against retro, which is what this is, right? I mean, joss sticks, hello? Don't tell me you've been doing this nonstop since the summer of love, Sky. Anyway my hair's not long enough now.

Me, I'm staying low profile till something breaks, here or back in Atlanta or New Mexico. A job, a house-sit, whatever, an internship with a newspaper. I'm housesitting now for an acquaintance, through April. The wrap's looking wonderful, Alison. Tight. This Sky's had some experience, one can see. Babs's and Katie's too, you girls'll wow Cleveland. You seniors? Juniors, okay.

I've lived in Key West for twenty years off and on, mostly off. Once I drove a pink cab two years. I've seen changes, let me tell you. I remember when there wasn't one tee-shirt store on Duval. Pedicabs, we always had those, although I've never pedaled one or even ridden. You girls catch sunset today at Mallory Square? The fire eater there's an old friend of mine. What music you like? Tex-Mex, salsa? Gangsta?

Funny things happen in Key West. You wake up with a stranger in your bedroom. An intruder saw your open window and dropped in. Probably doesn't harbor particularly sick thoughts, maybe only theft, but in Key West even theft is, how shall I say, flaky.

I knew a woman had her dog stolen, mutt, one afternoon vanished off her front porch floored in that fiesta conch style with broken tile embedded, black, pink, seafoam, and some kind of fifties lemon. Black mutt with a moustache going prematurely grey, moustache like Mutt's, or was it Jeff. She put up notices on telephone poles, waited, finally gave up. Eventually an old conch lady from around the block brought the dog back. Claimed it had wandered into her house but of course she had stolen it and kept it leashed. Otherwise it would have found its way home, dogs can.

Dogs can even tell when their human is about to have an epileptic seizure, and run for help. Don't worry, I don't suffer from the falling sickness. My cane's for balance more than anything else. I have an inner ear problem, cochlea. Sometimes I can't even hear myself think. Who knows, maybe there's a sword concealed in the cane, it's thick enough. I can always pretend I'm blind if I need to halt traffic, or I could beat off a mugger with it.

Did your parents name you Sky? You must have friends say, that Sky, he's the limit.

In the embrasure of a store merchandising adult toys and videos Sky sits on an African stool, lanky, fifty, ginger and freckly, in an overall. Alison, an odalisque between his knees on the balding kilim, and her chums disposed nearby watch pedestrians, bumper-to-bumper automotive traffic, an open trolley, a white stretch, a dune buggy riding its own carpet of green neon, cyclists, pedicabs. The three pairs of doe eyes never meet but stray to the street, to Sky, to Megga. She, fifty, pale in faded black, with incipient pouches, bruises, chewed nails and lips, short lank mop like a terrier's. Staring Granny Smith eyes. Wears a squash blossom brooch, worn Reeboks, Ray-Bans, walks with a thick black cane atop whose crook she crosses paws.

Megga slides her Ray-Bans up onto her crown. Down at the corner the pedimented clock always reads twelve-thirty. Sky holds the strand of Alison's luminous black hair in his left hand and with his right wraps one of the twelve lines in six colors around hair and floss, banding a column half the diameter of a soda straw that runs from the cardboard guard to his precise and strong brown fingers. He has wetted the floss between his lips. Behind the plate glass behind him an armless hollow pink fiberglass female sports leather and chains. On a ledge near her shoulder stands a semicircle of vibrators each in its own ice-cream pastel. On another shelf lie four magazines.

This particular wrap is European, Sky explains,

smooth, no knots. As opposed to Katie's American style, whose knots raise a low relief like a vein spiralling the tube. Megga resembles Queen Victoria. Sky doesn't know who you'd credit his name with. It's the tail of the Walter Sbynsky he grew up as and still goes by to the Feds and Big Blue. He could make Sky legal but as a rule he's never been one to capitulate. He schmoozes on, more lowdown about hair wrappers.

—Most are young dudes, some women, mostly men, twenty, twenty-three, and most wrap for a living. Some sleep on the beach. They sleep easier now it's legal, I imagine.

Couple or three learned wrapping from me. I learned it in Oregon back in the mists of antiquity, the dimmy past. I've done it more lately, now demand's up. J & P cotton embroidery floss. It shrinks a bit and tightens. Some skeins have five-strand floss, some seven, some eight, it varies. You find them at sewing centers or Woolworth's. The colors have numbers, not names like paint, but I employ them like paint.

I begin with half an inch of two colors in a fine alternation, a flicker I call it, that anybody can look at and say, hey, Sky wrapped this, there's his trademark. Variations are infinite for all intents and purposes.

Take branches. You divide the shaft say halfway down into two or three for a tassel, maybe each branch with its own pattern.

Tightness matters as much as anything. If the wrap loosens anywhere, the whole thing will unravel. Maybe I braid the hair first, but not necessarily. The little single hairs peeping out along the column? Loose ends. You try to preclude them by choosing hair the same length, but some strands break, it's inevitable. I trim them back with these special scissors, although you can zip a Zippo down the wrap if you're careful. Key West is pretty permissive, and I wrap hair without a street vendor or cosmetology license.

—Cosmetology? Megga gulps air and shifts weight. Is that the one they call the queen of sciences? Or maybe that's scientology, or economics or something.

Nowadays colleges teach everything, self abuse, you name it. Back when I was you girls's age we weren't so career-tracked, and not everybody automatically went to college. Especially not girls, unless it was nursing school. Myself, I considered nursing. Secretarial, too, but you can tell when something's not right. It seemed okay then not to go to college. I had a spotty decade in Arkadelphia, waitressing, clerking in a florist's.

But I did go to college for a weekend, when I was a high school senior. An Arkadelphia boy was a sophomore at the university in Fayetteville, and he invited me to come for a fraternity dance. He said a coach and his wife would let me stay in their guest room during the weekend. Sky, I'll bet you were a frat boy somewhere. Maybe the same fraternity if I could remember its name. No, it was different.

I borrowed a ball gown, strapless pink tulle shading to charcoal at the hem. I stained my white pumps as near the same pink as I could get. I took the Greyhound to Fayetteville with a grip and an overnight bag. Sterling picked me up at the bus station and drove me to the coach's house.

The coach's wife, small and brisk, breezy even (they must acquire it from the athletes) wasn't quite the attentive hostess I had expected. She showed me to a maid's room and then left without a word about dinner. Plus there were two beds in the room, and one had luggage and a movie magazine on it. Imagine my consternation.

After a while I went downstairs and rooted around

in the kitchen. The house was empty. I made a meat-loaf sandwich and went back up for a nap. Sterling wasn't to call until eight, but at six I had a rude awakening. My roommate returned from an early supper with her beau. She was a high-schooler, too, from Little Rock. Class sweetheart or mountain laurel queen, with dimples and corkscrew curls, and more, er, development than I had then. Vera Pruitt. After-ward I saw an ad for her father's Little Rock plumbing company.

Vera explained that the coach might not know Sterling from Adam. The coach was just a sponsor for the frat.

It turned out to be a double date. The frat house had pretty streamers, and a live three-piece band played waltzes and jitterbugs for a while. I could tell the tutti-frutti punch was spiked, so I contributed half of mine to a windowbox.

Around about, well, about this time, the four of us took a stroll in the garden. Not to put too fine a point on it, those boys started to get fresh, and not in any hesitant way. Worse, Miss Pruitt demonstrated a readiness to comply. An eagerness, even.

Megga stares. Sky nods as if to say, it takes all kinds.

The whisper of a glance passes among the three pairs of grave almond eyes. A spectator smiles.

—I insisted on being returned to the coach's house then and there. Vera never came in. The next morning when I went down for breakfast, the coach's little daughter presented me with a bill for the use of the room.

It was a weekend of misunderstandings. Who knows, if it hadn't been so strange, my life might have headed in another direction altogether. I might have married, and never driven a cab. I might be a grandmother living in Arkadelphia instead of Key West.

Er, do institutions of higher education still have frat weekends for girls like you three to enjoy? College boys inviting hometown lovelies? Not that I was exactly lovely.

Passersby covered in jangling idiosyncrasies dawdle for the sheer theater of the hair wrapping, and some confer about availing themselves of the service, yes let's, or rather maybe on the return, there's so much else to see. The warm night moves like breath. The gathered audience shifts, and a portion drifts away across Duval.

Now the gathering parts, and through the opening shambles a decrepit spectator, plop plop, his nose hanging down one side of his face, something like an eyeball pendant on his other cheek. Fingers at the ends of his lax arms wave like eyestalks. Short, eighty-ish, says wonder how much that sweetie-pie charges, to let you play with her hair like that.

No doe seems to register, but Megga harrumphs almost to herself. Not blinking, Sky asks, who says this is play?

But the unfinished heckler says, wonder does she charge more if you do it in private? Or maybe it costs more for the public fondling, wouldn't be surprised. Akimbo and ragged, the teeth in his petulant mouth reek. A rat's tail, looks like, dangles from an ear. Then again, he says, maybe the surcharge is for having it your own way, whichever that is, unless it costs more to have her take charge. And do the three come as a package, cut-rate? Seems to fumble in trousers pocket, waits.

Strollers laugh and converse in English, German, Spanish, Japanese, French, Eastern and Eastern European tongues. Pairs of pairs off the cruise boat docked in the bight, many ages, sexual orientations, skin colors, now and then a child. A boy on a motorized scooter, an actual scooter. A school bus painted white passes like a ghost ship, dark inside. Out its windows hands wave, "Sky baby," Key West hair wrappers and friends leaving tonight for the New Orleans Jazz Festival. Megga went once back when she was drugging and drinking, doesn't recall much. Sky never, though this year he would have except that he's been put in charge of some of the layoffs at IBM Boca. Besides, somebody has to stay behind to wrap hair. Independently Katie, Babs, and Alison observe the dumpy Megga and the weedy Sky, the passing pedestrians and dogs, the pedicabs and cars in the street, the bicycles, the sidewalk performer up the street pretending he's a statue. They watch and listen in peace, with all the time in the world.

—Let me know, Alison, if there's any discomfort as we work our way along. No charge for old what's-his-face, the itinerant entertainer. I should bring him back to Boca to announce the layoffs. Maybe he could spin them into desirability, know what I mean, Megga? Had him a snoutful I think. We mix it up once or twice a month, him and me, but I don't begrudge him his air space. Too much love on this street for that.

Matter of fact, if you young Clevelanders happen to work up class reports on this trip you might mention the Rainbow of Love, some twenty of whom this week are gracing Key West with their presence, camped at Higgs Beach for the showers and grills, and of course the ocean. Some show here on Duval after dark, for entertainment and also to accept offerings, food, cash, hair wraps. I wrapped one earlier this evening.

No, not Krishnas or New Agers or anything—they don't seem to be bankrolling anybody, and as for faith, they don't seem to have any quick fix. They claim to live without earning wages. IBM's dream labor force, you might say. Only kidding.

Supposedly there are a couple thousand nationwide in the group, which dates from the sixties, ancient history. The ones here now are newer recruits, in their twenties, although the one whose hair I wrapped tonight told me he's second generation, conceived at a Dead concert.

Every couple of years the whole tribe congregates for a solstice or equinox. This spring it's in the Florida panhandle. The ones here are an advance party.

Don't ask me any more about them, doctrines. I must say, though, I like their vibes, and I might consider signing up if I were younger and freer, readier to kick over traces. Ever known any of them, Megga? Supposedly they scavenge garbage to supplement handouts. Most of them look healthy, though.

Yesterday morning they created a bit of a scandal over at Higgs. The tide was high, and all twenty waded out to waist-deep. They held hands in a semi-circle and chanted a blessing for the island, including all of us, I imagine. A patrolman cruising by freaked. Before you could say Jack Robinson there were three patrol cars, blue lights flashing in the dawn. Bullhorns ordering waders out of the ocean. According to my wrappee, the charge was holding a public demonstration without a license.

Megga shrugs.

—The law's the law. I mean, were you there? How can you be sure it was a blessing they were offering? Anyway, who do they think they are, blessing us? Maybe we're blessed already, or some of us might prefer damnation, or at least noninterference. You say they're harmless, but I ask myself if it's really such an open and shut case. For instance, why couldn't they perform their blessing in the dark? Oh well.

—Easy there, Megga. We assume hearts are good

until we're proven wrong. Right, Alison? So, Katie, Babs, see this loop in the floss? Watch it disappear back into the tube. And now a snip, and there's your wrap, Alison. Check it out in this mirror. Right, four bucks for four inches, and here's your change. Enjoy what's left of your stay, and come back to Key West. Send your friends down, I'm sure they must be good people. Night-night, girls, night-night.

With a hand mirror Alison looks into the oval mirror Sky holds behind her. She sees the completed wrap, orange shading to pink, pink to orange, fluorescent against her sable locks like a thrilling bolt of thought. Alison nods and lays folded bills, discreetly as she has seen her father do, in Sky's dish of offerings. Katie and Babs stand. They admire Alison's embellishment, and each other's. Alison stands.

—Well, well, says Megga. She applauds and three, now four bystanders join her. Ears rosy, Katie inspects the tip of her own wrap. Alison sights down the street where her father should soon appear. Following the glance, Babs glimpses a man displaying an albino python. She links arms with Alison and Katie, and the three set off.

—So what was I saying? With fingertips Megga

drums a tattoo on her forehead, thrip thrip. Oh yes, how many will you be surprising with pink slips, Sky, and when did you say the ax would fall? I was thinking, since some of them might find the moment opportune for a career shift, your avocation might become their vocation. You could show up here with a squad of Boca trainees, hit Duval and spread, blanket the street, exterminate competition. Then diversify. I've often thought there's a niche here for cotton candy (blue's my favorite). As far as that goes, some of you might turn the odd dollar unwrapping hair. Seriously, though, what kind of severance cushion will these layoffs have? Not that it's any skin off my nose. Yours either, I guess.

—No man is an island though. Sky sighs. Now he seems to wink. No lady either, hunh?

Megga purses her lips —No island is an island, not anymore.

—No anything. But these employees, they'll get fair severance, and some won't mind the dole. Plus we're only talking eleven layoffs. Still, two are married to each other, with a couple of kids. Some have house payments and they all have car payments. They'll pinch. I don't look forward to giving them the news, even though they expect it, and Boca, well, there are worse places to be homeless, if it should come to that. Bosnia, Fargo North Dakota.

I had to lay a crew off year before last, and you do what you gotta do. But it won't be easier this time. Worse, because I know these ones better. Also I'm older and the empathy kicks in stronger. The thought's crossed my mind just to quit. Let somebody else dirty his hands.

—Sky, you got kids yourself? How about family values then, you got them at least? Tell you what, you're going to survive this personnel contretemps. Pour yourself a stiff margarita tonight up in Boca, kick back, check out *America's Funniest Home Videos*, Bosnia. Surf the Internet. Take it from me, Sky, you're coming through this one intact.

Myself, I actually have fond memories of Fargo North Dakota. I grant, you wouldn't want to sleep many winter nights on those sidewalks.

Here stands the pale dumpy Megga, owlish. Maybe she hasn't bathed recently, her shins look soiled. Smells a bit like peanut butter. A denizen, genius even, of the here and now. Her black cane something she roots in garbage with and then rinses the tip of in a public john. Harmless but not precisely anybody's cup of tea just now, if ever. Here sits the Sky dispensing wisdom and beauty. Wrinkled and whiskery, neck grainy. Wants out of his life, and who knows, maybe he'll find his way down here. The deep tropical night sighs flowers and ocean and exhaust.

Sky winks with both eyes. —Catch you next time, Megga, and give you a wrap for yourself. Don't want the distraction, I'll give you one on the back of your head where you'll never see it. And a price you can't refuse, say zero. Just a thought. Ornamentation seldom hurts. Calling it a night, are we?

—First, sometimes I take a stroll by the water. Funny you don't wear gloves, though. Me, I'd worry about communicable disease with so many people's hair in my hands. But maybe you develop some kind of immunity. Okay, toodle-oo, Sky. Nice to make your acquaintance.

—So who's next then for a hair wrap? Don't coast through paradise with nothing to show for it. Yonder lady with the cane, I nearly persuaded her. With a Skywrap she wouldn't look quite so defeated. We all benefit from a touch of enhancement. Look at the underbody neon on that Packard.

Look at that foxy pearl gray Packard floating past on its bed of violet light. Behind smoked glass you can distinguish shadowy driver and passengers, motionless, doubtless gawking. A zone of silence surrounds this automobile. The neon does it, the suffused violet silences the car and the environing glitz. Not that the light exactly deafens you. Rather the neon violet under the car divorces sight from hearing, and leaves sound behind.

—What's this, an innovation? In front of the old San Carlos Opera, Megga pauses among spectators arrayed about the living statue. He has established a niche for himself on Duval, and he earns a good take from tourists and other passersby. A truncated Corinthian column serves him for a pedestal, atop which he poses like a god or hero, powdered all over to a marble white, chlamys, skin, nails, hair.

In the past the statue has simply held still, and seemed not even to breathe, as the crowd kibitzed and tried to make him smile. Tonight, however, one of his arms has shot forward and its marble hand encircles the wrist of a careless spectator in her twenties. Enjoying the game, she glances at her boyfriend, laughs, this is fun. But what is she meant to do? She looks up brightly to the statue.

His hyacinthine locks might really be carved marble. He holds motionless his very eyes, which nevertheless see between whitened lids. Soon, however, he will have salted away enough profit for white contacts that will perfect the illusion of sightlessness.

▼

They fly down to Biloxi for the January character festival, and for yummy shrimps. Known one another forever, never better. First morning the instructress whoops all seven seminarians like chickens out into town. Gather ye traits in this delta sunshine. Lucille coos, the waterfront, Elmer, grab us a cab while I primp, and don't grouse, snookums. Elmer sighs, donning his porkpie. In his view preliminary inquiries at the visitors' bureau might be more prudent but oh, all right. From a pocket of his checkered vest he retrieves his whistle.

"Excuse us, Madam," he says to the driver. "Couldn't help noticing you haven't attached your seatbelt. Where we come from, there's a law."

"Here too, but I have a hernia the belt irritates."

Elmer raises his eyebrows. Lucille purses her lips and nods.

The waterfront hums. Crowds, children, a gator wrestler bubbling with fun, a smirking tomato hopper, wrens, one puzzled, gulf oilsters and boilermakers, Betty, Tommy, and friends, Giordanos, vacuumcleaner salesmen, shrimpers, garlands of cherry-red bird peppers, tear-stained parcels. A long sweep of sailors, no end of humanity. Lucille accosts a tugboat captain. "Age?"

The captain pushes back his hat to scratch. "I should say anywhere from 55 to 70, Miss. I've been with her for 37."

Elmer cuts an eye at the tug, and Lucille comprehends. She tells the captain, "It was your own age I had in mind, actually. But that's neither here nor there, and indeed you look to us as if the same answer would do. We're in town for the character festival, this morning sent out to see what we can bag. What did you say her name was?"

"'Was,' Miss?"

"Heh, heh," chuckles Elmer. The captain does have a point.

"Or is." Lucille smiles sweetly.

"She's the Moxie (of Biloxi), although I didn't name her myself."

Elmer harrumphs. "Shall we try a different tack? What might your favorite color be?"

The captain taps his pipe on a stanchion. "Got me there. I likes more hues than you can shake a peg leg at. But maybe I could name a worst favorite. Describe it anyway: almost grape, but with more brown in it, and some blackish rust, but blaring, mind you, for so dark a color. Me, I nigh barfs when I happens on it. Seems like it makes me smell shoe polish in the back of me snout."

"What do you collect?" asks Elmer. "Myself, I collect vintage computer magazines. Lucille here collects buttons."

"Me thoughts," says the captain. "Each morning while I struggles free of the dregs of sleep. Me dreams has allus been tenacious. Why, this very morning . . ."

"Excuse us, Captain," warbles Lucille. "To be quite frank, it's your character that interests us, rather than whatever it is that your dreams might be thought to reveal."

"The trouble with dreams," explains Elmer, "is that they precisely lack character. Not while experienced, perhaps, but when recounted, they're like peas in a pod."

"Dang nabbit," interjects the captain. "Shiver me timbers, that's exactly what me dream this morning concerned. We was in a typhoon, me in the mess eating peas. Couldn't for the life of me get that last one lined up on me knife blade. Just on the verge of success, me blamed bladder woke me."

Lucille bubbles, "Elmer here will certainly recall the squeeze I gave his hand, I believe it must have been, when we first glimpsed you sauntering down your gangplank, and I said, 'That man has character to spare, or I'm a strawberry frappe.' Elmer agreed, bless his heart."

Elmer shoos the butterflies away. A cigarette smoker with a box of popcorn feeds pigeons and gulls. Elmer says, "Suppose you weren't a human being at all. Suppose you were some kind of bird. What bird would that be?"

"I have a choice?"

Elmer says, "Er. . . ."

The shadow of a frown crosses Lucille's brow. "Yes and no. Just answer as quickly as you can, without giving overmuch thought to the matter. We're counting on you, Captain."

The captain squints into the distance. "Tell you what: I wouldn't mind being one of them ptooeydactiles. Come flapping over the horizon, drop a blasted mountain on some yacht, har har har."

As Elmer jots madly, Lucille observes, with a forgiving smile, "Mmm, wouldn't that make a nice splash! Except, you know, Captain, the question wasn't precisely what bird you might *choose* to be—"

"Assuming," interjects Elmer, now tucking his silver pen back into its holder, "assuming the rules are flexible enough to include your candidate under the avian rubric. Personally I can't recall seeing it stretched earlier than archaeopteryx." He tucks his jotting notebook judiciously into an inside pocket of his safari jacket.

Lucille pooh-poohs melodiously. "Don't strain at gnats, Elmer dear. As I was reminding our captain, the looked-for bird really wasn't the one one might enjoy becoming (for whatever reason), but rather the one

one would *be* if one *were* one, instead of what one actually is. But perhaps our feathered friends are too proximate."

"Using the term 'feathered' loosely," murmurs Elmer.

Lucille nods. "Not to mention 'friends.' So perhaps we'll strike pay dirt farther afield. Do humor us, my dear captain, by entertaining a condition contrary to fact."

"I'm all ears," the captain growls.

Lucille trills, "Imagine yourself a common household substance."

Elmer retrieves and flips open his notebook, slips out his pen and clicks it to active. "Or, if you wish, a common cabinhold substance."

"Wax," says the captain without a moment's reflection. "Good clean woodwax. When you pushes it you feels a momentary resistance, and then you feels it give. Seems like a kind of malleability comes over it."

Elmer and Lucille exchange glances.

"Ask me another," says the captain.

Lucille and Elmer hesitate.

"I'm all yours," adds the captain.

"Hmm," muses Elmer. "We might risk tiptoeing

into the abstract. Let's say you're a number instead of a tugboat captain. You've always been the one and never the other, ever. It's as though you were born a number."

"But I weren't born a captain, unless by extension."

Lucille gurgles, "Oh, forget birth, Captain. Just say you've been a particular number from the beginning of time, one among the swarming possibilities." She eyes a scuff on the toe of her gleaming pink left pump. "But not one, since I've already mentioned it."

"Odd or even?" asks the captain.

"You tell us," encourages Lucille, glossing the toe against the back of her right legwarmer. "Big, small, even, odd, integral, irrational, one has your name on it. Quick, which is it?"

"I fear you has me over a barrel now. Numbers was never my forte." He squints at the sun above a steeple. "Ten bells, mates. High time for yours truly to shove off." Slings his squeezebox over a shoulder. "Chug a lug for me this evening." Saunters into the sunny crowd, end of the squeezebox sashaying.

Elmer shakes his hands in the air. "Whee!"

Lucille claps hers. "Heaven! But who takes credit for bagging him, Elmer?"

"Pshaw, why not the both of us? Indeed, I see no reason in the world why we shouldn't work as a team for the rest of the day. Shall we, for once?"

"You're on. We're sure to be pressed about the number issue though, no? Should we prepare an analysis? Here's mine. I may have made a tactical error when I ruled one out. In my view, he thinks of himself as number one."

"Possibly. In fact, probably. However I can't resist offering a different explanation."

Lucille leans toward Elmer. "Mmm?"

"Should we have put the question to him in the opposite direction?"

Lucille leans away. "Don't go cryptic on me, Elmer. Take me with you."

"Maybe we should have asked, if a particular number might have been this particular tugboat captain (instead of a number), which number that would be."

"Oh dear, Elmer, you've made my head spin with that one, sweetie. Because, well, what would happen to all the remaining numbers if one of them became . . . well, you see the problem. Whereas if one human being drops out of the race, no particular difficulty. Even one tugboat captain."

"I have to hand it to you this time, Lucille. Incidentally, which number would you yourself be? No cheating, now."

Lucille considers. "Oh, six or eight. A streamlined eight perhaps, or even nine in an odd sort of way. You?"

"Guess."

"Oooh, I love it. Let me see. Um, um, um, how about a clue, you wicked child?"

Coy Elmer offers, "It starts with a p, at least in English."

"A p? Was our captain dreaming about this number's initial then? Hmm, a p. Paradiddle isn't some kind of a number, is it? Too bad we don't have a dictionary handy. Wait, wait, I think I have it, Elmer. It's pi you'd be, isn't it?"

Elmer shrugs. "Bingo."

"You bowl me over, Elmer. It's you to a t."

Through eleven, noon, halfpast, under herds of Biloxie's famous sheeplike clouds woolly in their eye-blue sky, the duo pursues the slippery prey of character. Manner a hop, skip, and a jump away, if yet not quite the thing itself. The chambermaid throws open bedroom windows, gingerly the sleek banker steps out of his limousine, the ragamuffin squeaks like a toy. Likes and dislikes count, habits, tones of voice, head-gear, any other of millions of indices. Notebooks bursting, the pair wheels into a southside hole-in-the-mall, itself reeking with character, for u-peel-'em shrimp bucket chowdowns and brainstorming. If dogs have character then why not children? Or maybe they do, a childish one. Which comes first, the character or the quirk? But dogs, Lucille's poodle, Elmer's Aire-dale back home, each in its way a real character, loaded with characteristics. The Airedale (Danny) lightly ar-thritic, the pearl grey miniature Bootsie a bit of a biter, both pedigreed to be sure. If only they could talk or, come to think, count your blessings. Shrimps to die for, coleslaw, hushpuppies, sweet tea dimpling and weeping down the striped glass pitcher. Topped off with mud pie slices well slathered, yum. Elmer always the dandy runs silver comb teeth across his scalp. Lu-cille refurbishes her maraschino pout.

On, through a scudding afternoon, cabbing, stroll-ing, for every dud a find. Both now using electronic notebooks, intrusive yes but further scribbling on the congested paper pages risks tipping everything there over into the illegible. Finds, nay trophies—the stocky hyperthyroidal cemetery gardener, her grubby digits tamping loam around a late pansy set as if proofing dough, as she complains of her cousin an ex-mayor, ferociously though not quite plausibly, how he blew her dowry, a trove of nineteenth-century Dutch winter landscapes on his second campaign, where-upon her intended decamped. Many races and racial mixes, many chocolate and golden postracials, every age, gender, mood, every degree of felicity and heart-break, new coiffures and old, there for the savoring and probing and for the unfolding to other seminar members and the instructress between four and six back at the Gulf Collegium Artium, now in the glass conference hall cantilevered over the waves. Each member or team displays discoveries on one of the sloping trays about the walls, and then the instructress shepherds the entire troupe around to ponder the day's results.

"Ponder," Lucille confides, "whenever I hear that word I think of 'The Wayward Wind,' a popular radio song of our youth, Elmer's and mine anyhow. When I was six or seven that song seemed the epitome of po-esy. It was about someone who spent his younger days in a lonely shack by a railroad track. Maybe Patti Page sang it. For some reason I misheard the refrain. I know you'll think me a dodo when I tell you. The refrain said that the wayward wind was a restless wind, a restless wind that yearned to wander. Which I somehow misheard as 'That yearns to ponder.' I don't think I had any very clear idea of what 'ponder' meant—maybe in fact it seemed to mean something not unconnected to 'wander,' but more mental, a kind of mental wandering maybe. That haziness made the word all the more rhapsodic for little me. Perhaps it was Frankie Laine. Anyway whenever that song came on the radio, I dropped whatever homework or play I had in hand, to swoon around the house singing too, barely able to wait for the refrain to come around again, so that I along with Frankie or Patti could deliver myself over, transported by that terrible yearning to ponder.

"Eventually I noticed my error, or it was brought to my attention. I could hardly credit the truth, it seemed so to detract from the song. For a period then I listened intently, and skeptically, when I heard the song, hoping to find the correction erroneous—not for the sake of my own dignity but rather in a sense for the song's, as I saw it. Live and learn though, 'wander' it was, no two ways about it.

"So then the song slipped off the charts, I slipped into adolescence, and whenever I happened to recall my error, it was as something mildly shameful and laughable, an instance of a childishness I had put well behind me, safely behind and now could smile at sophisticatedly. The world turns though. I seem to have outgrown the yearning to wander that once felt like part of a sweet core, and imperative—I did my share of wandering, too. But in riper years I sometimes find myself transported more by an actual yearning to ponder, to ponder deeper than I've ever done or ever will do. It's a rather more poignant yearning, for obvious reasons.

"Well! I for one am ready to schmooze."

"I didn't want to interrupt," breathes Elmer, "but, if I'm not mistaken, the singer in question was Gogie Grant."

Around the handsome conference table the seminarians by turns elaborate on their harvest, and on how it has changed them, what taught. "Some," cautions the instructress, "may have labored under the misapprehension that today's exercise was competitive. It was not." Elmer and Lucille eye one another discreetly with a mixture of relief and disappointment. "Except," continues the instructress, "in this restricted sense: character partakes of the ineffable, so that we can only compare notes within reason and, though your victory may not appear, still you may always outstrip anyone, including of course yourself." Lucille and Elmer study their hands on the wood before them.

As it turns out, the duo have constituted one of two teams at this year's festival. The other, a young trio of tidewater Virginia post-rap musicians, African-Asian American brothers and the Slavic-American wife of the younger, call themselves The Spirit Catchers. Their presentation leads off. Despite the drummer's stammer, they make a showing Elmer calls "creditable if a trifle lackluster," in his minute fastidious script on a festival notebook sheltered by his porkpie and Lucille's duffel from all eyes but hers. The Spirit Catchers propose treating character as behavior's melody, the analogy suggestive however feeble their exemplifications of it.

Next up is a New Orleans dentist for whom character manifests best in the buccal cavity. He gives a riveting account of peering as if into very hearts in his office. Tongues, he explains, tell little. Waving and lolling almost as if of their own accord, they distract and may seriously impede the business at hand. In the best of worlds, he opines, we would do without them and he would have unobstructed views of each unique enamel and silver colonnade, and of the equally distinctive ribbed firm pink vault and softer bluish floor and pinker softer walls.

Lucille and Elmer in their turn redact their day's catches and distill each to an essence of character conveyed in a lapidary detail or two, as with the oafish gardener's chapped lips, the boilerplate jollity of the tugboat captain with his plum suspenders.

Finally this year's sole debutante, a famous ravishing Laotian poet in tulle, down from her home at the Iowa Writers' Workshop, maintains that, seated, the human body broadcasts character with peculiar amplitude. As she talks in her thin monotone, a certain circumspection passes over her seated auditors.

"Well done, all!" The instructress radiates approval.

Elmer raises a plump hand. "If I may, before we adjourn?"

With a discreet though not quite surreptitious glance at her tiny wristwatch, the instructress allows, "Please, please."

"It did occur to me today, sometime, perhaps on the waterfront or, if not, perhaps at lunch when Lucille and I were wolfing down some of your scrumptious swimps (as I believe I once termed them), that we today have been not unlike hounds tracking elusive prey. Which figure," Elmer adjusts his cuffs, "compounded itself. I mean that, as I envisioned doggies loping hither and yon, noses to the ground, the olfactory dimension came to seem a rich analogue for character itself." An utterly discreet sniff. "That is, odors present themselves almost directly to the brain, if I'm not mistaken, each in the most florid distinctiveness and recognizability. Marcel Proust knew as much instinctively, though he failed to understand that most 'taste' happens in the nose. So then character may behave like scent in our mental negotiations, if you see what I mean."

The instructress's stiff smile slides upward. Lucille whispers "mental negotiations" as if happily committing the phrase to memory. The Iowa poet's jaw infinitesimally drops but her hauteur persists. Gnawing knuckles, the New Orleans dentist summons all his dark blood to his pocked and oleaginous face. The Spirit Catchers elbow one another.

"It's simple, really," continues Elmer. "I think we can all agree that even the richest templates of character—say the twelve types astrology provides—are monumental simplifications, and yet at the same time the characterological array isn't a complete congeries either. No, we certainly note many overlapping similitudes."

Elmer shakes his head wonderingly. "The situation can induce a certain silly helplessness, an aporia if you will. Whereas it appears to me that we have a reassuring analogue in odor, a suitably rich realm, with thousands and thousands immediately recognizable and also, I hasten to add, subject to any number of classifications. Just think for a moment, when was the last time you smelled an odor like none other?"

Lucille rocks back and forth, considering. "The electricity in my building went on the blink last summer, three days in July. No air conditioning in the middle of a heat wave, imagine! No elevators. And it wasn't just my building, it was the whole neighborhood—which for the first two days deserved the name, us all helping each other, sharing candles. But on the third day patiences started wearing thin. Well, as that period progressed you can bet I was subjected to some odors I'd just as soon forget."

Elmer nods. "And perhaps had managed to forget after some prior experience?"

"Possibly. But when power came back on, in the middle of the night noise and light woke me with a start. I sat right up in bed. Out of the vent near the ceiling were coming the first gasps of the resuscitated air, and with them something that smelled quite novel, so strong it seemed to be making my eyes cross, and thereby disagreeable of course, yet also, how shall I say, commanding, and cleaner than clean. 'This is how electricity smells,' I thought. 'If I put my nose into a bouquet of electricity, I would smell this.' It seemed new."

One of the Spirit Catchers emits a low whistle. The instructress frowns as if to force her smile back into place.

"A counterexample then," says Elmer. "Well and good—bluffs are made to be called. All the same I believe my point stands."

"Ahem," says the instructress.

The poet has slipped a microphone from her valise, and now she aims it at Elmer. "Your point," she intones.

"Mercy me," says Elmer. "I'm sure not to do it justice if you're recording it for posterity."

The faintest flicker of acknowledgment crosses the poet's face. Her mike waits.

The dentist says, "Rise to the challenge, man. Bite the bullet. Anyway, posterity? What's it to you? And who's counting?"

A different whistle from behind the teeth of another Spirit Catcher.

Elmer brings together the tips of his fingers and thumbs, spread in an airy vault. "My friends, my friends. Let me put it this way. With odor we get along very well without any overarching taxonomy. Why not similarly for character? You know? Or, if you prefer, here's a similar analogue: faces, with all their idiosyncrasy. I suppose a certain common denominator may be abstracted from them but . . ." Elmer holds the pause, his belly jouncing with a chuckle, ". . . but so what?"

The instructress bridles. "Do you mean to deny the existence of rules of character? Tricks for pinning it down?"

"Posit as many as you wish or need, for heaven's sake, laws, techniques, ploys, whatever. Incidentally, now that I think about it, odor is the better analogue for character, better than face, at least in this one respect: while with face it's possible to construct a kind of common denominator—of the constituent shapes anyhow—two or three dots above a line, the configuration even newborns respond to, if I'm not mistaken—I believe we would find ourselves hard pressed to point to any common denominator for odors and scents."

"Smellability?" asks one of the Spirit Catchers.

Unperturbed, Elmer says, "Ah, but that's vacuous, isn't it? Or circular? What's lacking is something that all smells could be reduced to, and that could be smelled itself. I venture to suggest that the situation with character is similar, and that we might be better off recognizing as much. But enough of my ditherings." He beams. The poet's mike disappears.

The instructress springs to her feet. "Ditherings smitherings: every contribution counts. Now then, we recommence tomorrow at nine-thirty sharp in the mollusk room, with talismanic objects, and with totem animals chosen in advance."

Lucille checks her wristwatch. Down here the dusk gulf light holds deceptively, going green and horizontal through the glass room. Lucille and Elmer dawdle as out file the instructress and their fellow seminarians. "This room," sighs Lucille. "I think I'd come to the festival for its sake alone. The architect's celebrated, isn't she?"

"Deservedly, although her name seems to have slipped my mind. So, eight-thirty at the Endless Shrimp? Time to change? Meet you in the lobby at eight? My treat tonight."

Lucille rocks slightly from side to side. "Sweetie pie. But this room, Elmer. I was thinking it's like this past year. We always thought of it as the first of the new millennium, until we found ourselves in it, and learned that in fact it's the last of the old. It's seemed precarious to me, this peculiar year, as if projecting over the next millennium like this room over the waves. Didn't you always secretly suppose you wouldn't make it this far?"

Elmer says, "Absolutely. Here we are, though," and he plants a light peck on Lucille's cheek.

ICEHOUSE BURGESS

▼

I grew up in a Kansas City icehouse, loving dogs with their furry muzzles when they'd sniff past the ropes and peeling posters of a morning for a wad of sausage casing, or even a handshake in the dank gloom where the duffers and me slung steaming blocks onto the loading platform straw. I did love those teary-eyed mongrels more unconditionally than I've ever thought to love any human or other vertebrate, not to mention anything else. Kansas City's good licorice, wrought iron fences, brass chugging the topsy-turvy woodwinds, they echo deep down the years.

Don't fret. Memory bides its time, until a dislodged engram floats up, of betrayal or great harm. Can it be? Traces coalesce into what will soon subside and be lost again and perhaps forever—a coarse imitation of a stammer, a poinsettia fallen off a corner table, exposed roots shivering above the clay shards and sphagnum, points of foil fluttering in the air.

Neighborhood strays would pitter-pat across the threshold and peer through the weak light at the winches and tackle, maybe trot over to sniff the rim of an ice pit, alert as tourists and as oblivious to differentia like the absence of ceilings and women. I think I loved them absolutely. I wouldn't have died for any of them, but I might have wanted to—whereas with people I've loved (and some others too), while I might on occasion have given my life, I'd have hated doing so.

"Boy there, Budgikins lad. War bells be tolling, the grainbelt needs ice for its catfish, boy. Shoo that tick hound out the alley and get yourself back to spreading straw. Milk'll spoil, think of the butter sunning without we keep these mothers moving." All true—then as now I saw veracity without blinking—and so back to work. Fido, you're on your own.

Later me and the Missus resided on the rancorous

coast, what seemed a lifetime, twice procreating (Lily T., a state senator in later life, or so it seemed likely, and Eugene D., long since deceased), me bootblacking to amass a bit of a nest egg, in the Hawaiian shirts that became my trademark, until branching into hardscrabble options, snarking virtual promos, a bit of this, a bit of that.

Years fly. For our silver anniversary I bankrolled the Missus to a nail salon in Newport News, something she'd dreamed of, and struck out on my own again. Since boyhood I'd fancied disguises and now I'd feed my humor for as long as it took. Animal trainer, private dick, mogul, sanitation worker, arms dealer, Saint Nick himself once—I moved about the US and dipped into the Caribbean or Mexico. In a given locus, depending on my mood, I might settle into a hotel, lay duds out on the bed, wait till the downstairs staff changed so as not to give consternation, and hit the streets. Or in a particular metropolitan area I might rent an abode for six weeks and enjoy a score of disguises, or even only three or four, each maintained days.

Were this another sort of story we'd now have details about how it could all be managed—as, insurance? They may fascinate in and of themselves, no question, and lend credibility. The world runs on such satisfactions. Here, though, other aims rule. Trust me. Think electronic transfers, de facto residence, portability, graduated fees, medical web shortcuts: things took care of themselves.

No one ever penetrated any disguise of mine, for how could it be possible? I made minimal social contact—petting a leash of corgis, snapping a mugging before it deteriorated, I could let diction and accent go hang. On rare occasions some exceptionally acute observer narrowed eyes, alerted by no more than a withholding of commitment or assent, that may've left me a minim smaller than was to be expected, a shade less prompt.

Thereabouts, when the winker started popping up with nary a by-your-leave, in virtual terrains and in what we called email, I was as much in the dark as anybody. Put me in mind of the old *Life* promo to introduce the screen doll a trifle salaciously, "Raquel is coming." The winker had the same piquance for me. Surfing a call-girl net, I wasn't surprised to happen on that eye, where it seemed even more inviting, and specifically female (imagine that). The chemical spongiformatives it proved to be advertising being irreversible then (seems only yesterday much "was" irreversible), and me cautious as a feist with turning meat, I declined, nor have I indulged since we've had reversers. You never know. Give the long-promised permanent reversers a decade, then we'll see. I can hack oddity, and vision. Focusing costs more each year, but distinguishing what's in focus grows easier, and more automatic, even when (I must admit) more of what I distinguish disheartens me.

In a dusty eucalyptus grove in a quake-prone mesoamerican lullaby or crumbling capital, me a donnish surveyor, I came upon two particular people—and one or two others may have been there in the cool striated afternoon. The two reminded me of forest birds addressing one another, the way they pushed the curled leaves this way and that with their feet.

Call them A′ and B. In a glance I saw A′ as like a wild elephant recovering from a narcotic dart to find herself noosed, shackled, and shouldered by cousins born into captivity or domesticated. Older, shorter, sleeker, B—"Brainstem," although not without cunning—had just finished a shrug that said it was all the same to him. Had I stumbled onto something illicit souring? I set up my tripod and sighted wide of them, needlessly because they took no notice of me.

Absolutely no notice, because one of those instants had started that can last forever. For all B's mock diffidence, the same nightmare honey had englobed him as A'. When it ended (if it did), the loser would quickly consign it to oblivion, and so the winner, if it was B—another day, another notch. And if A'? Well, victors may fail to weigh victories, for many reasons. But now, I could tell, for both of them this yawning instant felt graver than life or death.

I may have conflated details, and transposed the incident from where it really took place—a lobby dolled up for the winter festivities, say. There'd been a rash gesture. While a bellhop carts off the poinsettia, its poisonous roots quivering in the air, I in my porter's uniform (twill, cord passementerie) locate a dustpan and whisk broom for the blue glass tree ornament shards scattered on the marble, leaves from a bonsai eucalyptus. I take my time and eavesdrop. Relax, Burgess. Don't be so hard on yourself, here, let me sweeten the deal, what's the diff?

You wouldn't understand, avers A'. Mistakenly, I think, for it seems to me that B needs capitulations, and takes holdouts as threatening his own bargain. At the same time I must say that now, even if time again slowed precipitously, here with jingle bells and sleigh bells, busy faces, I felt half tempted to parrot B, say go on, get it over with, you know you will in the end. The dustpan opened its maw as to say, it's history, nobody gives a shit and anyway it's not your life you're signing over, more like the next week and a half, after which you can renegotiate. Sure now, I almost agreed, and there's pleasure to take from casuistry too. But I didn't intervene.

Quit stalling, says the Missus when I got this far in the story. What with this and that (including an infarction) I'd thought it was time to ease my show off the road for a breather. The salon still bumbled along, and next door she'd opened a tavern. Fair draft, darts, waterfront trade. An old salt or two evidently wanted into her pants but she wasn't having any, and she welcomed me. I caught up on the skinny on kids and the odd friend. The KC icehouse had finally been mulched, she'd heard, and that cost me a pang. Her dog Gus, part wolfhound, welcomed me as if I belonged. While she tended bar I'd play my mouth organ in the back booth, Gus's muzzle on my lap, or trade yarns with habitués and drop-ins.

Cut to the chase, Budgie, says the Missus, rinsing glasses. Gus on the floor against my stool rattles his collar. A younger limey concurs and wants to know what is it with this prime anyway, why not just plain A? Bite the bullet, mate, he says, we're dying of suspense (my own money's on B). The Missus's upper arms have lost some of their heft, and they seem to have dried. She squints through the middle band of her trifocals, encouragingly. One night I could drop in here bedight as a marine biologist. She wouldn't catch on, at least not for a while—or even if she did, either way it's a lark. I could bring my latest trophy, an undreamed-of species in a plastic bag, and set it on the bar for all to admire its fins like stilled fireworks, its swivelling unconcerned eyes. You'd know me, Gus, but not blow my cover, would you, boy?

All ears the half dozen that hoarse February eventide, one a matronly regular from the salon who allowed herself the odd luxury, new poinsettia nails drumming an inaudible dead march down her gin fizz. The tavern can feel cozy but it didn't exactly feel that way then. Nobody'd lighted the gas log in the hearth. They didn't forebode, the pickled eggs, the filmed mirror, the mounted elk head, but no more did they comfort.

Okay. As for the prime, put it this way: it leaves elbow room for A there, who might be the same, or maybe not after all. (With B, why bother?) "A'," as if the story might have come out some other way than it does.

So I started to bite the bullet and once started I barrelled through to the dismaying outcome, how A' had folded—hunkered down, signed on, lowered sights, there are a million names for it. I'd watched A''s face brighten with the relief of letting go—I could see it felt like a renegotiated mortgage, a gusher of means from nowhere. There was but the merest twinge of awareness of another construction for the choice, itself irrevocable and more consequential than A' would now ever be able to know. I told how as I stepped away (B already having bid his avuncular adieu) and watched A' diminish in perspective, a trick of the light made it seem possible for me to glimpse into the thorax and see the heart swell and thin like a paper lantern.

Personally, began one of the gobs, ready with commentary—he'd seen stranger things, whatever. More prescient, the Missus cut him off. She didn't recall hearing the tale, and wondered had I told her it in days gone by, or anybody for that matter. No, I said, this is the first time it's passed my lips.

We're honored, mate, began the gob. Once again the Missus intervened with a good question: why now, Budgie?

Had to get it off my chest, was all I said. Yes but why now, she might have persisted (I could have shrugged, something in the air), or even just, yes, but why—but tending bar teaches you when not to persist. In the silence, whose awkwardness seemed sensible even to Gus, for he woofed under his breath, it began to dawn on me (at least) that the time had come to strike out again for parts unknown, and that unburdening myself of the story of A' and B had served to trim me for travelling lighter out the last third of my allotted time.

What else might there be on my chest, asked the matron folding arms under her ample one, since we're in this mode, or maybe somebody else has something to share. I myself, she continued, have always considered myself a shoplifter, although I've never fallen prey to the temptation, quite.

The gob had been scrutinizing his suds. Just one question though, he said. Why A and, more particularly, why B? Anything there to do with your name?

Not a thing. A the first letter that came to mind, B following naturally, but it could as easily have been Z—except that (come to think) Z's too exotic for an epitome of banality. However you're welcome to assign other letters or names to suit your fancy or need—mine, yours. I scratched Gus behind his ears. He looked up at me while I did it. He liked it, and he knew I knew he did, but Gus wasn't a whiner, and when I stopped he laid his muzzle on his forepaws and took a deep breath, as if he divined my imminent departure and had resigned himself to it.

Some belt-tightening seemed in order so I bought a used van I could live out of. Will you be coming back, the Missus wondered. I said I honestly couldn't say but if she found herself in any kind of scrape she'd know I was only a message away, and her benefits looked dependable. She said, take care, Budgie.

I'd never seen the land of enchantment, New Mexico, so I went there for what I thought would be a month or so, but which lengthened into more than three years. In the high desert south of Santa Fe I found a landowner willing to let me park nights in his arroyo. I could have driven back into town each evening, but I wanted the quiet of the desert. Days on end I walked through the scrub cactus and tumbleweed.

Although this wasn't the territory of the Anasazi, the old ones, on almost every excursion I came upon their successors' arrowheads, some of which I collected and kept in a bowl in the van. Others I left where I found them. Sometimes when I stood motionless for a time, a prairie dog ventured to show itself. April, cool air and hot sun. With my good sense of direction I could take bearings from the Sangre de Cristo range, so I never got lost (not that I'd have minded much). If I had left the van at an offroad parking I timed walks to get me back to it before dark. When it was in its regular place on the other hand, I didn't mind walking home after nightfall. Such times the brittle stars in the high desert clear sky felt more distant than ever and yet realer too, as though they might rain down the back of my neck. I slept like a baby and dreamed like a child.

More precisely, the high desert air seemed to have blown my dreams clean so that they had a sharpness I remembered from childhood, even while the dreaming mind was adult. Waking, the aging and enchanted mind worked otherwise. My short-term memory began to fail, whereas eidetic moments from the distant past were apt to coalesce patiently and without warning.

Less pleasant was a new susceptibility to mood

swings, sometimes into moods I had no precedent or good name for, such as a particular groundless irritability against which I had no remedy. What would Ben Franklin have done in the circumstances, I strove to imagine, he having been a boyhood hero of mine. When eventually the very rapture of the desert began to annoy me I decided to move camp to a lower elevation or a city. Santa Fe had its attractions but finally the grittiness of Albuquerque appealed more, per se and also because of my budget.

Several disguises from the old days had stayed with me, in the van's aft locker. I tried my old routines but whereas before they had made me nearly invisible, now they drew attention. They were outdated, and also, whereas before I had taken pains with each detail, now I sometimes donned components of more than one disguise at a time, as if they were fungible, only to find myself the laughingstock of a band of schoolchildren—bear paws under the soutane hem, they were right to laugh. For protection I more and more became a night creature, even in dreams. I feared I might be losing my marbles.

Late one evening I found myself in a predicament, in a sixth-floor apartment I had haunted for days without the owner's knowledge. He had turned off the lights and left for an errand. As his elevator reached street level however (I could hear it), he suspected that his apartment wasn't empty, and immediately returned to his floor. As his purposeful steps approached down the corridor, I took refuge in a walk-in closet whose door stood open. I heard him stride from room to room. Weak light came on in the hallway. He walked down it and stopped at the closet, the only remaining place for an intruder. I watched his hand pass the doorjamb and approach the light switch reluctantly, as if he were telling himself at once, "This is silly," and also, "Okay, this is it." A horrible fear overcame me, a fear much more for him than for me, a fear of what effect the sight of me might have. All I could do was utter a strangled moan, which woke me from the nightmare. I felt elated, that my mind had taken me so near the face-off, and also regretful that we hadn't gone all the way. Then I listened. I'd parked on a back street but my moan could still have alarmed a pedestrian, and I didn't want authorities cognizant of my way of life, which I supposed illegal. But the only sounds were my breath and pulse.

Visual distortions led me to a brain surgeon who

showed me X-rays of a tumor big as a hen's egg, which had to be removed and biopsied quickly. I claimed to have no relatives or dependents, left a will in the van bequeathing everything to the Missus, and came back the next morning to go under the scalpel. The tumor proved surprisingly benign. There was no pain during recovery but it took me two months in a rest home to regain my strength. The day after the operation, however, my vision returned to normal. More importantly, so did my frame of mind, and I have never since been troubled by any susceptibility to annoyance or gloom. For a time I wondered if I'd been administered a mind-altering drug but no, simple relief from the tumor's pressure had returned my old equability.

When I left the rest home I rented a furnished cottage, isolated but more comfortable than my van, on a ridge northwest of Albuquerque, built fifty years before and inhabited only intermittently—by prospectors, I liked to imagine, although vacationers would be closer to the truth. Negotiating the dirt road was an adventure in the best weather, and in snow I didn't brave it. No power or plumbing.

The crossed snowshoes on knotty pine, the brass ashtray in the form of a coiled rattler might have been chosen a lifetime before as proper for a mountain hide-away. The bedstead had a niche in which a tenant had left his dozen paperback hardboiled detective novels from midcentury. The last book I'd read cover to cover must have been an abridged James Fenimore Cooper, *Lake Ontario*, in the library of the Kansas City orphanage I spent my childhood in, but now with time on my hands and no television, I let curiosity sway me. What first attracted me was the puzzle of the shelf order of the books, for it was not by author, nor by any alphabetization or any other rule I could conjure out of the flaking spines or from the lurid old covers with their blistering gelatin. Nothing for it but actually to peruse some contents, which quickly hooked me on the wistful preglobal locales and period murkiness. The shelf order rationale never revealed itself, but then I didn't concern myself with it after the first book or two.

Around this time I witnessed an actual murder, during a trip into town for provisions and a check-up by my surgeon, whom I liked a good deal, if I haven't already mentioned it. I'd found his face trustworthy from the first consultation, a Thursday the twelfth, so much that I hadn't balked at scheduling the operation for the next day despite my habitual superstitiousness. The murder, neither so glamorous nor so sordid as those I slept beneath, looked like a turf war episode, the victim a mere courier, the weapon a silenced automatic handgun. It happened outside an upscale Italian restaurant in a mall, and it dismayed me. Despite my age I'd never seen anyone die, much less be killed. The victim was falling forward, flailing—but soundlessly, as if the pistol's silencer had operated on the target—and the next instant a corpse lay not ten paces away. And yet it dismayed me less than A''s capitulation to B had done, or even the two or three deaths of dogs I'd witnessed in my life. Why? I'd loved the dogs and, as for A', that had seemed a prognostication of what could be expected of "fellow" creatures.

When I'd got back on track I celebrated my recovery with my first visit to Europe. More precisely, to the part that had attracted Franklin (because of his name?). As with New Mexico, what looked like a brief visit lengthened. I didn't know French but I'd picked up some Spanish in Albuquerque, which now seemed to morph into French of its own accord, like an animal adapting protective coloration. In Paris the Mona Lisa looked more disapproving than in her pictures, and the Eiffel Tower looked solider in person, so I risked an elevator to the top. At used book stalls on the Seine I bought a pocket bilingual dictionary and a "polar," a French equivalent of my New Mexico paperbacks, from the same era, and I made progress with it during quiet evenings in a postage stamp room in a postcard hotel, evenings spent there to economize, and because I felt that my age had begun to make daylight hours more suitable for me. I found the polar softer-boiled than its US analogues, and less innocent thereby.

I couldn't be sure, though. Codes for the illicit —drugs, untaxed luxury goods, and works of art— escaped me, some anyway, in the novel as in the Paris streets. My habit was mildly to decline whatever seemed any sort of invitation. Similarly I declined three unmistakable invitations from prostitutes, although I did go so far as to inquire about prices, as an excuse for having a moment of observation. One of them was young and pretty, but I doubted that even with her my old peter would show much interest, and for mere conversation the rate was more than I wanted to pay. But I could note her sweaty perfume and cigarettes and her ankle bracelet at dusk in the Bois de Boulogne.

Other appetites banked too. In Paris of all places I
had to remind myself to eat. Although my budget shut
me out of nine-tenths of the city's restaurants and
brasseries, still I could have indulged myself—on oy-
sters, for instance, the first taste of which had been the
gustatory revelation of my eighteenth year. But the
simple interest failed. There they lay on beds of sea-
weed and excellent crushed ice, with lemons, sized and
graded, fragrant as an impossibly fresh prostitute. I
peered at their rough white and verdegris. No, I
thought, I need something else, the heart changes. But
I did stand myself to a dozen *fines de clair* and enjoyed
them, and even enjoyed the verification that they in no
way assuaged the restlessness I had felt for weeks already, like an entirely mental hunger that I couldn't
pin down long enough to guess how I might satisfy it.
But I owed my poor body enough nourishment to keep
it working, and so I set myself a routine I've followed
ever since, of taking two meals however light every
day.

I left Paris almost on a whim, to see castles in the
valley of the Loire. I saw some of them in a weekend of
touring in a minibus. Those structures exhausted my
body with their ramparts and dungeons and winding

stairs, and they numbed my mind with thoughts of their histories. To be sure there were older artifacts in the world, and I may have seen older ones even in Paris. With these behemoths, however, sighing alone in the countryside or above a village clustered against the feet of their walls, age itself seemed to flaunt its intractability.

I'd meant not to stay more than a fortnight over here but I had a return ticket open for up to a year. Unexpectedly Tours on the Loire sank its teeth into me. It seemed far safer than any equally interesting city I'd ever set foot in, I liked its insouciant patchwork of the venerable and the merely outdated, and I liked being taken no notice of in a provincial university town. I had begun to adopt invisible disguises when the urge struck—they caused less trouble—and I enjoyed taking a coffee or a beer disguised as an impoverished young history student, ravelled scarf around and around my neck.

Several bridges span the Loire linking central Tours to Tours North and St. Cyr. One of them touches down on the Simon islet and here it was that, on my fourth day, I noticed what had been a campsite on waste ground under one of the bridge's arches.

What sort of person had stayed there, I wondered. A wino, a footloose and pecunious youth perhaps? Halfway across the bridge a pedestrian stair had led me down to the island, a municipal park to the east of the bridge and a restricted water quality testing site to the west separated by the bridge's footprint, a strip of "terrain vague." When I stepped off the stair onto the path that leads east up the center of the island (with ribs out to the circumferential path), glancing down the steep incline to the foot of the nearest stanchion I caught sight of a grey sunburst on the dirt, that had been an open fire—and then, near it, other evidence of habitation, a table and a chair and then, on the ground against the concrete, two more chairs and a crate. On a line strung from the stanchion out to the fence protecting the restricted area I seemed to distinguish two clothespins.

I strolled up the spine of the island to a bench in the sun, where I rested for half an hour watching the river's currents eddying about the outcrops of the island, before I returned to the stair to the bridge and so made my way back to the picturesque old town of Tours, where I took a plaza table for a lunch of a sandwich and a carafe of tap water. At the next table a cheerful trio of Californians winding up a semester abroad debated the fate of Oh-oh, a four-year-old griffon mongrel there with them. They had inherited him from their flat's previous occupants and wouldn't have minded taking him back to California except for the three-month quarantine. The invisible student disguise I was wearing that day made it easier for me to offer to take charge of Oh-oh myself.

The next morning I checked out of the hotel. Having left most of my worldly possessions in a dumpster, at a quiet terminal I transferred the bulk of my liquid assets into an electronic Swiss account I could access incognito. I bought myself a pup tent and a sleeping bag and a backpack and then swung by the students' apartment for Oh-oh and his papers. Having changed masters at least once already, he seemed to understand what was up and to accept it philosophically.

We proceeded to the Ile Simon site, where I set up the tent and set out food and water for the dog, whom I kept on an extended leash that day and night and for several after, until I felt sure he was habituated to his new life. He accepted it ungrudgingly, and I tried to follow his lead as, on the second night (before which I had been too occupied to reflect), the question "What have I done?" took shape in my mind. What indeed, for by then I had had myself smudged, out of official existence and beyond the reach (and ken, almost) of authorities and, it must be said, family. Oh-oh and I listened to the fat whirr of tires on the bridge overhead, punctuated by the dreamily soothing pitter-pat as they crossed expansion joints. We looked across the dark water at the city lights. We smelled cold smoke in the cavernousness, and vinegar, lichen, and excluded rain. All my life I had hankered for a dog, there was that. And it seemed to me that what I had now done also came down, maybe, to achieving a kind of irrevocability, an irrevocable freedom.

In ensuing days I half expected to be visited by the previous occupant whose vial and spent blood pump Oh-oh found barely hidden in high grass against the fence. I also felt "ready" for harassment. However, when the policeman who patrolled the park twice a day happened to find me at home we exchanged a few pleasantries and that was that. Nor have any young rowdies (if such there are in Tours) slashed the tent or thrown my scavenged firewood into the river while Oh-oh and I took the air in town, admiring Jeanne of Arc's armorer's house, or the Jardin des Plantes in neighboring La Riche, with its flowers and goats and ancient Mama Bear and Papa Bear, or the two-hun-dred-year-old cedar of Lebanon at the Musée des Beaux-Arts. I suppose that the realest if still distant threat (apart from the obvious one) comes from the capricious river itself, the longest in France and sub-ject to the rare flood high enough to cover my island.

Oh-oh and I generally leave soon after sunrise. I tend to personal needs at the train station or some other public facility, he his fewer ones (no shaving) where the urge strikes. We return before sunset, while there's still light for housekeeping and to build a ru-dimentary campfire. Last week at this hour, or per-haps slightly later, in dusk (between dog and wolf), a figure resembling the singer Roy Orbison, with the same dark glasses, came to the edge of the incline and looked down at us thoughtfully. The next evening he appeared at the same time, and this time after a mo-ment he made his way down, digging in a heel at each step. Here's trouble, I thought. Oh-oh watched me for a cue.

I seem to have guessed wrong however, for he in-troduced himself as a battery-powered print journalist coveting the story that had brought me here, and willing to pay what price I might ask. Nothing against your line of work, I said, but no thanks. Why not, he wanted to know. Well . . . I said, well, no thanks there too. He said okay then, so be it, and he made his way back up the hill, now sideways, never having shown me his eyes, nor have I seen him since.

Today Oh-oh and I returned well before our regular time, and strolled the accessible shore of the island, me in my grey sweats, black sweater and loden duffel coat, with vocal running shoes protecting my dreadful dogs, all beneath an invisible Ben Franklin costume replete with ventral padding and a double chin. At the prow, were the island a dirt boat, we sat on the ground where a bench should have stood, my back against a retaining wall. Oh-oh likes to fetch and he chewed hopefully on a branch we had found. If I lobbed it into the water, would he be so foolish as to leap in after it? I scratched his broad head.

The water of this deceptive river seemed to divide into equal currents washing either flank of the island. Their flow gave the illusion that the island itself was progressing—and yet to where? Up this long river as it gradually proves too narrow for even this small island that, even if it could slough and scission, would at length find itself high and dry. Progress in the other direction would entail unmooring the island, to coast out to the wide ocean. Better continue proceeding upstream, I thought.

Before moving I entertained one further reflection of the sort I find myself prone to in these days of narrowing prospects. I've mentioned the experience of having French seem to give way to English, as if under sufficient attention the language trembled and assumed a more legible state. The same, I supposed, might happen with the visual field at some moment— say this vista of water approaching from under other bridges, with human settlements on either shore. In my remaining time, though, such a revelation seems unlikely.

In a few moments Oh-oh and I will bestir ourselves and proceed down the port shore, slower than the water, enjoying the view of the complex pontoon of the right bank with its moving toy cars and trucks. On our public spot we'll sup and settle in on for the night. The morning he wakes to find me rigid, he should have the presence of mind to go looking for a kind soul to tend to us both.

▼

Queer quiet warmish mid-spring, clear morning, wide weather, radio said a stationary front that smells like pewter. Glossy avenues north of the business district if not south, past the rush hour and into the quietus, not far from the decaying heart—between it and the first bypass and shopping centers—washed streets, bungalows, trees in leaf. Through sighing neighborhoods Cooper pilots a souped-up roadster from another decade, plashing across gleams and iridescences eyed like peacock trains. Misty silvers wiggle into the happy storm drains.

The city's new dumping ground lies hereabouts, more convenient than its predecessor out past the animal hospital, out toward the sewage plant. Not five months ago Cooper ferried a kaput printer out that road to the old landfill, on a crisp autumn afternoon —before they finally ploughed, spread, and seeded there, to let the tract steam through the mild thin winter as Cooper resigned from data management, gave up alcohol, signed on with a clinical PR agency, all the while following the state basketball rivalry, the crumbling of the old Soviet Union, and other plights (homeless, dying) through this nagging winter as he managed more or less successfully to shrug off his chronic incurable tendency toward a depression that if humored even through a single drear late-night cable uncolorized forties or thirties second feature with fur collars and a swimming pool in the apartment building basement, even with so little acquiescence his gloom will mushroom faster than can well be imagined—universal vacuum swelling in its first nanoseconds—and poor Cooper, nothing for it but to shove the heavy old printer out the hatchback, pay the fee, drive home and hunker down through an airy and tentative winter, leaving coffee grounds and cheese rinds curbside, orange peels and possible pizza under the transformer in the alley until now, spring at last glimmering everywhere and two grocery bags of personal papers beside him in the passenger seat, heading for the new waste disposal site hereabouts.

Not where you'd expect it, for these bungalows look recently lived-in, and here's a tricycle, a doghouse, though the terrain does heave up the odd uninhabited stretch, as here ahead. Cooper sighs and slows although nothing seems easier than proceeding straight down this unmarked asphalt past the last lawns into . . . a wet arboretum or public thicket of some sort, or more right of way condemned by eminent domain, for the stave of power lines stretching over the treetops to the next derrick. The far overpass must be the beltway, but no access or intersection in sight. With a second thought or two Cooper is contemplating a U-turn when what must lead to the dump opens on the right, unpaved. Lucky he's slowed.

Thus without overshooting and having to backtrack—something Cooper dislikes—he eases off into the muddy rutted lane marked only by an international refuse symbol on a post, stamped aluminum in reflective urine. This stretch will need widening and paving if the city expects to make more than token or cosmetic use of this particular site. Oh well, thinks Cooper, his own life or curve could do with a spot of maintenance itself. Tires squelch, a hummock growls against the belly, better pull off here where they'll eventually lay out parking, and a bunker-like guardhouse may replace the derelict cabin that might once have belonged to a forester. Angle in here beside the rusting Vega that might have belonged to the woodsman, shut down, slide out the grocery bags, lock up.

Might better have backed her in, and farther. But why, after all, Cooper thinks—why court disaster with precautions that would probably prove needless anyway, if not useless? Cooper strides away from the parking area like a first mate on shore leave, in dock shoes (waders if he'd foreseen all these bright puddles), white boxers under stovepipe blue jeans, a white tee shirt, and a lemon poplin windbreaker. Like handlebars Cooper's cheekbones cut the cool wet middle Atlantic piedmont air and it stirs against his pale cheeks and under his ears as if to coax out echoes of marine ancestors in tidewater Maryland and the Hebrides before, in invisible wind prints, and under each arm a heavy grocery bag of papers rests against Cooper's thin ribs. Away from his roadster and the junker, and the other car now visible, Cooper proceeds down the rutted lane.

Cooper's cousin Nate would have demurred from this errand, and maybe have advised Cooper to demur too. You don't look for muggers in Vail, where Nate's managed a condo six years now, but crime is everywhere any more. Nate said he knew he didn't know the dude that showed up one Sunday morning in the laundry room, and Nate knew the dude didn't look quite right, but Nate had his guard down from partying, and the dude drew a pistol. Couple hundred cash, some plastic, and the anorak Nate was tumble-fluffing. Where Nate's concerned, the loss proved his rule of thumb: minimize risk. On the slopes, in the futures market, steer clear of anything sticky.

Cooper and Nate aren't close in either sense, but they manage a weekend every couple or three years. Neither's married and though they never talk together about sex or love there are cars, real estate, movies. Nate would have advised against a solitary expedition down this muddy lane. The foliage will look smeared with gluey light later and drier but now, wet, leaf after perfect leaf might just have been cut to shape and hung out.

The slurping lane leads Cooper around a willow oak large enough to hide a tree house somewhere in it, bottles and galoshes strewn over the roots, and now the vista opens and the city's rationale becomes clearer. The open land stretching away in both directions like an abandoned golf course is in fact the right-of-way for power lines strung from derrick to derrick high above the rough sward the city, unable to improve, has wisely opened for dumping.

Nothing much here under the power lines humming in the lucency—bottle caps and such oddments, scraps, bones, ribbons and what not strewn among clumps of old wild dead grass and some green sprouting through, but little refuse. A child's buggy, some sardine tins and soup cans, pop bottles, remains of a campfire looks like, a softening egg carton over against the boundary.

Squelch, squelch, Cooper marches thither and deposits his grocery bags. Gazing down at the patchworks of thermofax, printout, and vellum, he feels a qualm about abandoning private matter here on this public ground which, come to think, looks oddly un-

derused even for so new a facility—until he shrugs.
His leavings will attract others, and before you know
it humus and much else will cover these personal doc-
uments.

Cooper feels something like a smile struggle up
from his innards to his face. How incriminating could
any records prove anyhow nowadays? And criminy,
Cooper reckons, hoosegow or chain gang, should he
prove liable in all innocence, why even then the better
part of his life has been his own to spend, so screw it.
Without a backward glance he tramps back through
the tall light across the rough to where he entered this
clearing, presumably.

Except that through here the light looks somehow
more nasal than before, and the rutted way less snivel-
ling, or is it a trick of the moment? Hidden birds un-
pack their hearts to the trees and air and Cooper. Birds
sing like tires squealing in another neighborhood.
Birds chink and twerp like bright gears dancing
through graphite. And the roadster, around this bend
Cooper looks for it in vain.

Wrong turn then?—even though Cooper seems
merely to have retraced his steps like a child in a fairy
tale or a hero in a maze. What could be more straight-

forward? Yet here ahead in a sort of bay thrown into the margin of the forest, a lone playhouse or one-room cabin (could be a childhood clubhouse), seemingly abandoned now, shaded by an apple tree in blossom, dabs of ice cream along the boughs. Cooper smiles. In the lambent air bird song clinks, and bliss from another time falls out of the apple branches, spreading.

With the knuckles of a curled hand, narrow wrinkled palm facing him, Cooper knocks cursorily as a monkey, and now in a moment he finds good light inside, empty wood shelves, and a dryish air. At the far window squats a utilitarian (and much used) yellow desk. Cooper sits on it. Out this window he sees rivulets snake under tires, box springs, and a refrigerator left there in a shaded gully, illegally then of course. Out these windows, and these, the boundary of trees and clumpy grass diminishes in either direction under fresh sky, and at the doorway light floods onto the threshold. The land below stretches away in all directions, even to distant cities Cooper has visited for business or pleasure and always, always, slid open drawers in case a previous occupant might have forgotten something, and never, never found anything left behind by accident, but only directories and scratch pads, and not even the cheap bibles that as a child he had riffled through for codes and treasure maps, always hopefully despite his unremitting bad luck.

Now Cooper sits on this desk in this abandoned cottage, ankles warming in a gloss of sun, the splintery desk top edge impressing itself into the backs of his thighs, jogger's hard lean thighs each with a narrow hand at rest on the denim where it lies with narrow spatulate digits, nails gnawed to the quick, pads weightless on the cotton. Cooper bends left, right, in the move he used first in boyhood to clear his ears of water after swimming, and now uses instinctively to stretch.

Months may pass. Outside not minutes away a nondescript murderer tastes a fresh amanita, fatally, and fortunately (need it be said?) for Cooper. So too out the windows and over the trees, behind blue sky blackness stretches, Cooper knows, farther than the eye can see, with swirling stars and dust.

On an impulse Cooper gives the drawer by his left calf a tug. Inside, *My First Stamp Album* bound in faded red flaking leatherette, that opened on the lap proves foxed, mildewed, and not altogether empty.

Cooper turns through persistent or erstwhile coun-
tries' pages of indicated spaces punctuated with roto-
gravures of postage once attainable by the neophyte
philatelist—a zeppelin, a pundit, the crescent moon
—and on the eleventh page trembles an actual stamp
thin as its glassine hinge. It limns a conical orange
tree, the tiny fruits visible among the dark leaves.

Moldering beneath the album lay several magazines, and now Cooper lifts them from the drawer.
Two prove story monthlies. A line drawing enhances
each title, and after a page or two each saccharine or
lurid tale breaks off to be continued later in the magazine, and interrupted and continued again, and again.
Toward the back, certain of these fetching accounts
break off, to be continued only in a later issue.

Cooper tracks one narrative from its historiated
initial through the pages as it appears and disappears
like a river coursing now below ground, now above—
a tale of cat smugglers—until it too dives out of sight
under a lure for next month's continuation atop a pha-
lanx of classifieds down the column, prim personals
and ads for a wrinkle cream and a hairnet.

When Cooper turns over the back page he peruses
the cover of an old comic book, Superman touching

down on a Metropolis street. At the left under some sort of thick white C serving as a logo, a table of contents lists the hero's three adventures to be found inside, these seriatim and complete, each ending where it ends even though, come to think of it, the protagonist's recurrence softens conclusions and commencements and turns each separate tale into a chapter in his life or career. Cooper sniffs the soft paper—old soap, lichen, and indeed the color of shower scum shows between the action-packed panels and rises through their Easter-egg washes.

Cooper lays aside the comic and regards the last periodical, a sex magazine of photos of bodies and body parts, and sex toys, bedding, ferns, and ancient telephones. He considers the brash actors in their intricate poses, and the beefcake knowingness or solemnity of their common youth, common to them anyway, or most of them, once. Hard to guess how many might survive, given the indeterminate lag between the snaps and the appearance of the magazine, itself of uncertain age, in strip cinderblock adult outlets.

Cooper's fingertip slides across a pictured nipple to the margin. He leafs farther, past untold shades of flesh with intervening uniform grey text. Now and again one cast links three or four photos with a touch of implied story—here a wink, here a sodomy—and these narrative traces touch Cooper, offered as they seem to be like lifesavers. He folds closed the magazine and returns it and its fellows to the drawer, that croaks and barks when he shuts it. His fingers linger on the pull—there, there, boy, relax.

What would cousin Nate make of this suspended morning? Medicinal savvy Nate who laughs like a sitcom, thumbs tucked in galluses, he might say, keep moving, dude. Change or die.

Much virtue in that "or," muses Cooper—there's a conjunction to write home about. Still, old Natey does keep moving. Cities and cities away this very minute Nate might be bobbing and weaving up a corporate fish ladder, barely showing whites of his eyes in any professional or marital loop. Whambam and outta there, grizzling as he drops stashes, flextime vacation homes, grandchildren, lingoes, on his way out to a leisure village and beyond, IRS never even close.

Ah well. Cooper flicks a smidge of lint off his elbow. He boosts himself off the desk and crosses the pulsing interior to the doorway. Hebridean and ready, brave Cooper takes the full wash of virtual noon in a wet empty spring, and the transverse sustained chords of the power lines, and birds winking and gulping, and all the perilous and meandering bright flood. He takes it as instruction (of all things), for good if memory will serve and at all events for now: don't capitulate, Cooper. Do not even dream of changing this life of yours.

Power lines zoom across the clearing. Yonder past the far rough, down a culvert squirrels scold the dwindling remains of a murderer, at a gasoline can rusted to stiff brown lace. Birdies peep and twinkle all through the brush and limbs environing the new dump. Farther, where habitation resumes, a child comes out to roll a toy truck over the wet grass.

IN THE MIND

▼

Years ago, when I was a young man, it was my duty to inspect a mind, my charge simply to make a brief tour and then present observations. I suspected that my learning might hinder me in the company of other men but, thinking it pointless to pretend to be of their sort, I dressed in a conservative suit and proceeded to the entrance, ready to meet reserve or hostility with courtesy. My guide, some forty years old, had spent his adult life in the mind. While he seemed amused by the whole business, he put me at ease with a respectful friendliness.

We rode a noisy cage elevator down a shaft cut in living stone. Odors of the man's sweat and of graphite lubrication for the winches made me lonely, for I was leaving behind the world as I knew it.

We alighted in semi-darkness on a platform at the intersection of several tunnels. It seemed quiet after the elevator ride, though I heard distant machinery. The guide lighted a torch from a pot of fire, and we advanced through the largest tunnel, its walls wet and alert as a dog's nose. I watched in vain for signs of ore, and in fact saw none during my tour, for it lay deeper than the level I explored. Beyond a depot where stood a line of dusty cast-iron trolleys, we emerged into a spacious chamber where a dozen men sat cooking at a campfire. I heard a tin can drop and roll on stone. As we drew nearer I saw past the fire a circle of spectators standing about a performer.

The men at the fire, ten and more years my senior, wearing faded denim and hobnailed boots, stood as we approached. The guide presented me and explained my mission—unnecessarily, for they expected me. These men's deference and even affection cost me the most difficult moment of the tour. As one extended his hand, I saw with some consternation that he had recently lost his fingers, so that sticky orange disks edged his palm, itself blistered and scored. I must have hesitated but I took his hand, and several others variously maimed and none healed.

I left the guide eating beans at the fire, and moved to the group of middle-aged spectators, who ringed a dancer not much younger than I. He alone wore no shirt beneath his overalls. As he entered the final stage of his stiff-legged dance, I felt a pang of sympathy for him, his fine thin body and whole hands, and his face yet free of his seniors' expressions and mannerisms; and the accident of our respective positions gave me some pause. He embraced me and led me down a tunnel where the firelight gave way to a suffused gray like dawn.

We passed alcoves and galleries dug into the walls of the corridor. In one, three men in respite from their work knelt around a game board opened on the stone. I watched one of the players manage, despite injured hands, to roll a die and nudge forward his counter with a portion of a finger. Stepping closer, I identified their diversion as the humble aleatory game of snakes and ladders. Other of the niches I peered into stood empty. A petroglyph on the rear wall of "His Master's Voice" represented a gramophone, and gazing at it I seemed to hear a distant tinny rant, with faint applause—echoes from greater depths of detonations and rock-slide, perhaps. In the recess called "Stone Tears," boulders hung suspended against the crag face, as if the men had so chosen to commemorate the melancholy of their lot, or even of the mind itself. I found myself recalling Virgil's *lachrymae rerum*, the tears of things.

To my surprise, at length the corridor opened onto a kind of underground universe. We looked down on a railroad track where stood a flatcar bearing a coffin of dull black wood strewn with dusty pink roses, perhaps because it contained a woman, that began to roll away, and in time disappeared in the distance. I waited until a proper train arrived, and boarded it.

I detrained in a Mexican village where lived a famous recluse, a collector and singer of folk music, whose work I had long admired. Presumptuous though it seemed to consider visiting his hacienda above the village, I had no alternative, for no life stirred below. I hoisted my luggage and toiled up the narrow winding streets.

A wall surrounded the buildings. I pulled a bell-rope, and soon the carved gates opened onto a courtyard, across which I saw the proprietor on a balcony. He smiled and beckoned me forward. Thickset men with machine guns flanked me, one took my luggage, and the other escorted me into the house. The musician greeted me and led me up a wide stair to a salon where tea was served. I did not question him about the armed men, nor did he mention them at once. For my part, I supposed them a simple necessity in what was then a backward and dangerous territory.

The musician had been born and educated in Madrid, had travelled widely, spoke excellent English, and seemed wise beyond his thirty-five years. I told him of my longstanding admiration for his work, and we conversed in some detail about a particular song. He was quiet, deliberate, and unassertive. Presently, without changing his manner, he told me that he intended to subject me to an experiment of his devising, and that until I complied I should not be permitted to leave the villa. Naturally I was anxious. That the experiment would be of a radical sort was suggested not only by the armed guards but also by my impression of the man's gravity. Still, resistance appeared futile and, since he seemed trustworthy, I signified my willingness to commence forthwith.

We entered an adjoining library where I sat in an apparatus like a dentist's chair with a cushioned head-rest. Meanwhile, the musician explained the experiment. He had discovered that he himself was able to look directly at a source of pure white light of great intensity. The same light had promptly and painfully blinded all animals to which he had subjected it. He believed that the effect on animals resulted from their inability to maintain a steady gaze. He intended to shine this light into my eyes. I would, he said, feel no pain nor lose my sight so long as I made no attempt to look away.

When I pressed my head against the support, the light source moved into my field of vision and brightened. For some thirty seconds I looked into the light, conscious of little else but the need to hold quite still. All was as the man had predicted. Soon afterwards I returned from the town as I had arrived, to where I had first boarded the train. There the mind now stood deserted. I retraced my steps to the elevator, which I contrived to operate, and so returned to the surface.

SCRUPULOUS AMÉDÉE

▼

1. NIGHT THOUGHTS

Clear midnight, calm sea. From his lighthouse on the islet Le Galiton, Amédée Conti sees an Arab crescent among quieter celestial lights. As white, reflections of his propane beacon shimmer on near dark waves. Low to the northeast the dark mass of La Galite, the island that is his home, where now sleep his mother and siblings and friends, and his wife and son and daughter.

Each ninety seconds Amédée's beam sweeps around across La Galite, sending gleams that diminish to invisibility but never die, Amédée imagines, east over the longest expanse of water, towards the new Palestinian nation of Israel, past the ghost of the great Egyptian lighthouse, around past Libya to the nearest mainland port, Bizerte on the coast of Tunisia that, under several names, has maintained loose control over Amédée's islands since before the realm of Carthage. The beam sweeps westward across the shores of Algeria and Morocco, where his father lies buried beside a coastal road, out to the straits and up around across shores of Spain and France, Sardinia, and Italy, land of most of Amédée's ancestors, and in past Sicily to La Galite three kilometers away.

Each morning Amédée rewinds stone weights and pulleys that turn the mirror he polishes each afternoon before he lights the flame and sets the gears turning. During the first hours after sunset fishing boats may pass on their way home to La Galite, and once or twice a week near dawn Amédée may see the Marseille-Tunis ferry. Twice a year some other vessel will pass in the night. As seldom, serious weather disturbs Amédée's quiet. There are Galitois tales of a leviathan apt to swallow ships in these waters, but Amédée has never glimpsed it. During the war U-boats patrolled here, and the wreck of one full of the dead washed onto the rocks north of La Galite, and stayed through four tides before the waves reclaimed it. This happened during Amédée's seventeenth winter, just before he himself went to fight and die, if need be, in Belgium. Now the thought of that time can give him a twinge of his private seasickness of the soul.

Amédée passes some of the night playing patience in the lantern room, or doodling on a slate, gazing out into the night. In the lighthouse, where he neither has company nor can bring himself to sing in his famous bel canto, he has no way to fend off his peculiar nausea when he feels its imminence, as now. Surfacing out of his thoughts, it can take forms so innumerable that he had no name for it through childhood and youth, when he rarely fell prey, nor later for a while until, because the sea often figured, and because the physical nausea waves can rouse could seem to invade his mind and spirit, he came to think of it as soulsickness, and it could be very bad. The beam turns above his head and leaks enough light for half-shadows in the chamber to waver and circle too, the dark blur under his hand as it hesitates over ten playing cards, numbered diamonds face down beneath king, queen, and valet, who watch him.

Amédée has thought to amuse friends on La Galite in the morning at Conchette's bar and grocery. No one will have gone out to fish because it's Sunday, and because the island has no priest, no one will go to the rough chapel either, and eight or ten will come to Conchette's. "If only some of you had been at the lighthouse last night for a game of *shkouba*," he thinks to say, naming the Galitois' favorite card game. "Luck had me under her wing." Hassen will be there, who usually wins at the game, and the Guera brothers who lose. Four or five men, two or three women including Conchette who neither wins nor loses when she plays, a child or two, and the odd dog. "With the ace through ten of diamonds, face down, my eyes closed, I'd move cards about until I had no clue what was where, and then ask a question. How many children do Carmen and I have? I turned over the deuce. I turned it back over and shifted the cards again. What is eighty-one divided by nine? The nine. So for half a dozen questions. Today's date? Six. When I repeated that question for good measure, and got a different answer, seven, I was relieved to have proved the cards fallible—until I glanced at my watch and saw that midnight had passed."

Some will scoff, Hassen will, but when Amédée swears it's true they'll begin to enjoy the puzzle. Someone, maybe old Silvère with a bit of coaxing, will think to ask whether the cards ever happened to give the wrong answer. Then it will be a good laugh.

It would make a good joke regardless of its truth, but Amédée has thought he can while away the night by enacting the story. The cards, more dilatory than he expected, have taken two hours to answer the first three questions correctly. Amédée sighs. Reduce the number of questions? "What's today's date?" In their second attack at the question the cards have offered nine, four, and four again like a refractory child. Amédée sighs, giving them another of what may have to be many more chances, and he turns over the seven.

He watches the red lozenges shimmer. After all, hasn't chance brought his hand to this card now, chance as pure as if this were the first time he put the question? If so, the joke he is constructing for his friends may be worthless. The joke may be on him. It seems a possibility one should consider.

Can't with impunity, Amédée has time to think, before he feels an insidious routine begin. Dread takes him, a dread of the flatness of his sea, and never mind the enormous ocean past the straits. That surface invites two orientations, the face down of the nine cards drowning before him, or the face up of the seven and the three faces, of the drowned rising. And yet—without turning it over, he raises one of the drowning cards to the vertical, the third orientation—there is an orientation for survival. Unless the horizontal sea itself should tilt, to stand vertical as in a map on a wall. "China face," say little voices. It only means the weight of thought on the other side of the world, Amédée tells himself under the turning beacon, the thought of human and not human beings there, allied by wakefulness to each other and to him. Merely that, and with any luck Amédée will recover his self-possession before dawn.

2. EARLY LIFE

The first of four children of Eugène Conti and Rose Cross Conti, Amédée spent childhood and youth on La Galite, helping Rose look after the younger children. During most of that time Eugène directed road crews around Bizerte and later in Morocco where (according to the document Rose received from a representative of the king) he succumbed to an ailment and was laid to rest. Amédée was eleven when the envelope arrived with a black ribbon caught under royal sealing wax. Amédée understood that he would have to shoulder adult responsibilities for the family more than ever, at least for a time.

Those responsibilities consisted mainly of watching over his brother and sisters, especially little Anne, tending the truck garden and the fig trees, hunting, and bartering produce or cash from Eugène's meager pension for fish and seafood at the island dock. Rose mourned a year, as a formality. She missed Eugène but he had never been home for long and, in any case, with four children she had her hands too full for self-indulgence. Tall for the island, and with a long face, Rose often as not gave vague or incorrect answers to questions and therefore islanders called her Linotte, for the forgetful bird—but it was never clear quite how apposite the nickname was, or whether some playfulness lay behind her unreliability. Amédée and the younger children humored her, much as she them.

Few clouds except for Eugène's death troubled Amédée's youth. There was no particular difficulty in the fact that, unlike most island men including his brother, Amédée proved even less suited than his father had been to life at sea. Amédée had the best will in the world and whenever as a boy he went out in a boat, he gave his all. However, as an uncle remarked, at sea Amédée moved as if dreaming. On land, though, Amédée was nimble for his large frame, surefooted over the rocks to the troglodyte school he and his mates sometimes attended. And handsome, never mind his lantern jaw, as the schoolmistress posted from Tunis remarked to Rose—it took an outsider to open the eyes of the community to a kind of beauty in their midst. Young Laurence, to be sure, already had her eyes open. As the island found Amédée desirable, she felt a secret pride, and some trepidation too.

Laurence needn't have worried, at least not right away. A year younger than Amédée, she had blossomed into vivacious adolescence a year before him, in time for him to be smitten by her pretty face and by her voice. Like him, Laurence sang memorably. They first made a couple in song, at school or about the island where their voices wove such ravishing duets, her sweet soprano trilling above his rich baritone that, as some said, they might have careers at the Tunis opera, or even La Scala. Amédée first declared his love freely in song, as did Laurence.

For a time Amédée in timidity held back from any more direct announcement. The first person to learn the state of his heart was not Laurence but rather his youngest full sister (Rose by then having remarried and begun to produce a second quartet of children) Anne, the sibling he most often confided in. On a rock on the high path from the bamboo grove thirteen-year-old Anne, already striking with her resemblance to the movie star Ava Gardner, listened like an adult. "What do you suppose I should do?" Amédée asked. He shook his large head as in apology.

"You must tell Laurence," Anne said. "I feel sure it's what she wants." Amédée seemed to divine some hesitation and he waited, but Anne said no more.

That very evening Amédée unburdened his heart to Laurence, and so began the two most purely happy years of both their lives. In long evenings spent in one garden or another, friends and relatives gathered to pass the time with guessing games and reminiscences, cards and dice, tales of animals and people and the beyond, in lantern light and moonlight when Amédée and Laurence sang an amorous duet old Elzéar might accompany on his guitar, a muted chord for each stanza. Conchette of the grocery and bar would nod in time with a faraway look, as if she could hear an undersong all her own. Eyes shone. The twining voices seemed to conjure a dream of great, common, enduring happiness.

Yet Laurence's parents held back, especially Philippe, rather like a commedia dell'arte obstructionist father, even though no traditional hindrance obtained. Some—difference of wealth or social standing —obtained nowhere on the island, nor did any ancient grudge divide these families. The best Amédée could make out was that Philippe, a good father, harbored doubts about Laurence's future with him.

Mending nets one blustery morning with a dozen other Galitois under a ledge near the landing, Amédée worked at Philippe's side. After an hour, at what seemed a propitious moment, out of others' hearing, Amédée asked almost offhandedly, "Suppose I were Laurence's husband. You'd wish she had chosen a fisherman, wouldn't you?"

Philippe cooled some but he said, "If it turns out she'll have to share a husband with the sea, so be it, but no, I wouldn't regret her having him all to herself."

Amédée tried to read the older man's face. "But suppose something about me troubled you, some . . ." in the loud wet air Amédée struggled for words, "some lack, or fault."

Philippe rubbed a thumb over his nethook. He said, "This isn't easy, Amédée, what you put me to." He continued, "Yet you have every right to know I feel uneasy about the circumstances of your father's death."

"Circumstances? But, but what can it have to do with me? And what can I do? He was a good man. I think you knew him better than I did."

A shadow crossed Philippe's face. He studied the nethook. "And there are your voices."

Amédée laughed. "I haven't heard them in years. Maybe I'll never hear them again. Anyway they did no harm." In childhood he had distinguished words and phrases in ordinary wind and waves, the creaking pines, the clicking bamboo grove. Islanders nicknamed him Radiola for a while, for the voices he could never make anyone else hear, and also for his own singing voice, as beautiful after it changed as before. It was at about the time of that change that his voices and their nonsensical words—"curfew forever"— became inaudible, as he admitted, and were eventually forgotten by all—except for Laurence's parents, it now seemed. "Radiola" itself fell into desuetude, to be replaced by "Cri-cri," for cricket, the musical insect, and as a roundabout acknowledgment of his sturdy size. Amédée laughed again. "Do me the kindness not to concern yourself with any of that—do Laurence the kindness." He looked away. "For the sake of my name, do the gods of love that honor."

Recalling the moment in later years, Amédée could never be sure about Philippe's reply. Possibly it was only a musing echo, "The gods of love," but possibly Philippe, a careful man, had in fact said, "The gods of loves," as if to correct and perhaps also to caution. The schoolmistress with a remark about the science of etymology had set Amédée to thinking about his name, and in time he had asked Rose where it came from.

"From me. Eugène left all of your names to me. He thought they shouldn't matter. But let me think." They and Anne and the younger children were husking fresh almonds on the terrace beside the house. "Oh yes, from my great uncle. A Savoyard, named after a Spanish king, if I'm not mistaken." Everyone listened: a king!

Amédée said, "What does the word Amédée mean? Do you know?"

Young Anne spoke up with great assurance. "It means that a god loves you. You remember Venus loved Enée? No, Maman?"

Rose nibbled an almond. "Yes, or else it means Amédée loves the god."

Amédée frowned. "Which is it?" he asked, a little queasily.

Rose shrugged and tossed the end of her almond to an attentive chickadee. "It's all the same, no?" She rumpled her son's curls.

Helpful Anne added that the name probably meant both, and Rose said, why not?

Amédée said, "I don't know about that. Maybe. But, which god, Maman? Is it Jehovah of the church of Rome?"

"Probably it is," said Rose.

As if his mother's vagueness weren't perplexing enough, in the following week it dawned on Amédée that his name might simply mean "God of love," or yet "Love god" or ". . . gods." The affectionate mockery in "Cri-cri" felt more comfortable. Yet Laurence always used his true name, and from her it sounded as if "Amédée" might signify her love for him.

One Sunday Amédée walked to Conchette's bar and grocery for a pastis and a hand of cards, and to purchase a spool of flypaper for Rose's kitchen. Having played an eight and taken four diamonds, he sipped his pastis and was returning the glass to a shelf behind him when he noticed, pressed against the table edge, the breasts of a girl four years his junior, Carmen Vitiello who, for as much as he knew, might have sprouted them the night before. She, intent on the card play and never in her life supposed desirable, took no notice of how her small full breasts lolled behind the cotton of her blouse. Amédée thought, good for little Carmen, and he looked up into the discreet yet direct gaze of Conchette behind the bar. Amédée half smiled, recalling how three years earlier Conchette, old enough to be his mother, had initiated him into the pleasures of the flesh.

So began a turn in Amédée's life that surprised him as much as anyone else. From that moment for nearly a year it seemed to him then, as ever after, that he wasn't entirely himself—not by becoming somebody else (although it might have looked that way, and some spoke of possession) but rather as if by a partial amnesia he had lost part of himself. "Carmen," he murmured, watching the girl's dirty elbow, her lank straw hair dividing over her neck.

Amédée told Laurence before anyone else that he

meant to marry this Carmen. Even so, he said, he had not stopped loving her, Laurence, and he hoped they would continue their duets—Carmen croaked like a frog if she dared sing. Amédée also hoped he and Laurence would remain lovers, whatever else happened. It was in the empty schoolhouse where they met after dark. She said, "Amédée, is this a cruel joke?"

He touched her arm. "No, Laurence, no. It is what will happen. I myself don't know why, and yet I know it will happen." He brushed aside the tears she felt on her cheeks. "You too must marry. We'll say you've fallen out of love with me. That you've seen I wasn't what you thought, that I'm . . ." Amédée searched for words, "wooden, and . . . empty."

Laurence laid a finger on his lips. "Hush, Amédée."

Amédée kissed her finger and then took her hands in his, between his knees. "For your sake, so no one will suppose the truth, and not Carmen either. It must be you who ends our romance."

Laurence said, "And then if Carmen turns you down?" But they both knew better than to count on that.

Amédée made the rupture known, so tactfully that no one could accuse Laurence of fickleness, and in due time he paid court to Carmen. At first she like others took it as a charade meant for revenge on Laurence, or else prosecuted out of some wounded bitterness toward all womankind. Wonder of wonders though, this handsome young man, the bewitching singer, really wanted her of all people, and in marriage. Carmen accepted, still half expecting disillusionment.

Amédée's own family, Anne anyway, doubted the official story. For one thing, Amédée seemed heart-whole and even cheerful in a dazed sort of way. For another, they knew him not to have been immune to feminine charms besides Laurence's. While she had no Galitois rival in song, there were other unmarried young women with recognized charms, but Carmen all too clearly was not one of that group. When Amédée told Rose and Anne that he had proposed to Carmen, after a moment Rose said, "Carmen will make a good wife and mother for your children." And she added, "And you'll know they're yours."

Anne said, "It's almost too late to change again, Amédée."

Amédée searched his sister's face. "Don't dream of such a thing," he said. He spoke quietly, and it seemed to Anne she could hear and see more resignation than resolve.

Amédée married Carmen in Bizerte on the mainland, where there were officials for civil and church of Rome services. They took a bus to Tunis, which Carmen had never seen, for a two-day honeymoon. Back on La Galite they settled into one of the houses that had stood empty since the early thirties when the island was more populous. A year after his marriage Amédée came to himself, after the long torpor in which he had felt rudderless and during which he had made the most consequential choices of his life. He thought maybe the birth of his son Antoine had brought about the recovery of his presence of mind and some of his happiness, and the birth of his daughter Marie-Rose gladdened him still more. His love for these children gave him a way to a kind of love for their mother, as if she in her utter trust were his child too. Laurence meanwhile had married and begun to raise her daughter Thérèse. She and Amédée continued to regale islanders with their songs and, as all knew, they resumed their sporadic meetings after dark in the school.

The world war took Amédée away to fight in Belgium. After a cursory training he went to the front, dreading everything about it. On the eve of battle a wave of nausea seemed to lift him off his cot into a sky crossed with rockets, where he looked down on ruined land strewn with the dead and dying. If someone else had married Carmen and fathered his children, he thought, and if the allies were the aggressors, he wouldn't have been bound to kill, or to keep from being killed.

As it happened, Amédée was captured before he had a chance to kill or to be killed. He spent two years in Germany or Poland (it was never clear which) as a prisoner of war. He and his successive cellmates enlivened the monotony with dreams of escape, and shared what they could learn of the outside world from censored mail. They suffered from malnourishment and some succumbed to prison maladies. A middle-aged Auvergnat gave up the ghost before Amédée's eyes in the yard. Amédée thought his own time had come when he developed a bronchial infection with wracking chills that only worsened under such treatment as the prison doctor could offer. When guards came with a stretcher he expected to be dumped into a potter's field or worse. What seemed a delirium of travel ensued. With a shudder he found himself in his own bed on La Galite.

Carmen brought a bowl of coffee. Apparently dying, he had been repatriated. Now, so entirely recovered that the illness felt illusory, and ditto the prison and the war (which ended within months), he learned that his stepfather, Rose's second husband Emilio D'Arco, had "gone to the hill." On the unsettled hilltop in question, Emilio had contacted people stronger than humans, and arranged for Amédée's safe return.

Questioned about his prison time, Amédée spoke of cabbage, and of how he had heartened others with songs, and of snow (which no other Galitois had seen). Amédée never brought up the subject himself though. When Anne asked why, he said, let sleeping dogs lie. The time felt incomprehensibly strange. In later years, as its enormity surfaced, Amédée supposed some glimmer of that must have leaked into the stalag without his knowing, and so estranged his life there. Even at his return there seemed to be more to the story, that he could never plumb. Part of it was simpler than he imagined, and less dreadful. Whereas all the houses he had ever known before were stone, the prison camp had been built of wood, vocal wood, and beyond its walls had stretched forest.

3. TABARKA

South-southwest of La Galite, near the Algerian border, lies Tabarka, a coastal village and an islet not three kilometers offshore connected since the late nineteenth century by a causeway. This is the loneliest part of the Tunisian coast. The nearest city, Bône where Rose was born, seems the more distant for standing in another country. By the time of the events related here, the French government had laid electric lines out to Tabarka to automate the lighthouse there, so that Amédée as keeper had less to do than on Le Galiton—a mixed blessing for anyone and especially for one given to speculation and susceptible to promptings that, he knew when he took the position, might be fearful here. But he needed the dependable and higher pay, with a son and daughter to prepare for the Galitois exodus already in progress that would leave La Galite deserted in a generation. And he needed dinars to send from time to time to Laurence, whose husband had been lost at sea not long after the birth of their daughter, and who at the time was scraping by as a cook down in Sfax.

When Amédée first took the Tabarka position he hoped to arrange for Rose (whose second husband had died by then) to visit him there so that he might accompany her west to revisit her birthplace. She seemed vaguely interested, and Amédée allowed himself to hope that, once there, she might be coaxed still farther west, so that she and he might at last view Eugène's roadside grave in Morocco. Nothing came of these plans. Rose's eighth child having reached school age, her health that had always been good began to fail, and precipitously, as if in retaliation for an excessive tour of duty, so that Amédée soon had qualms about not having stayed a bit longer on La Galite.

At Tabarka he lived in a room in a three-story hotel in the mainland village. He slept there through the middle of the day before cycling out to the islet, where he passed the night at watch. The last week in each quarter of the year a replacement freed him to visit family and friends back on La Galite, before returning to Tabarka, where he had no friends or lovers. He kept in touch with Carmen by mail, and a letter could take as much as two weeks. Mail moved faster to and from Laurence in Sfax. With the postal money orders he occasionally sent her, he included a word of news or encouragement, and she replied with thanks and kisses. Mail to and from Anne in Bizerte, where she lived with her new husband, a gregarious naval supply officer, could take as little as three days.

Carmen apprised him of his mother's health, as system after system failed. In particular Rose developed a diabetes that made her legs swell. The physician making monthly island rounds advised amputation which, he said, could give her years more, but Rose declined. She died two days before one of Amédée's returns, so that he had no need to apply for extraordinary leave to attend the burial.

"So, Amédée, are you finding Tabarka to your taste?" asked Anne's husband André, a natural *bon vivant* but now subdued like everyone else at the funeral banquet. He and Anne had left their young sons with friends in Bizerte.

Amédée smiled. "It's a good deal farther away than Le Galiton. And then the Tabarka lighthouse seems to be . . ." A still evening, under Rose's grape trellis candles barely flickering on the improvised banquet table around which the family—Carmen and the two children, Anne and André, other Conti and D'Arco offspring, with spouses and children—waited to see what Amédée was hesitating to say. He continued, ". . . it seems to be haunted." Younger eyes widened, while a certain disquiet passed over the adults: considering the occasion, would a ghost story be quite proper?

"This is news to me," said Carmen. "Haunted, Cri-cri?"

"Visited, anyhow. I learned it only last week myself. The night before Maman. . . ." Amédée frowned —was there a connection? "That lighthouse has an attic. Early Thursday morning, I may have dozed, and around three I heard, well, I thought it was my voices like before, over my head there, yet they sounded realer. Two men talking."

"How could they get there, Papa?" Antoine wanted to know.

"It didn't seem possible. I walked around to the stair and climbed it. I saw what I first took to be two old Arabs, in *djellabahs*, playing cards, *shkouba* in fact, and paying me no mind whatsoever."

"Were you afraid, Papa?"

"I suppose so, and yet they seemed to mean me no harm. They were enjoying themselves. Then I recognized one of them as the god Jehovah."

Grape leaves stirred overhead in the wondering silence. The god Jehovah. Finally Anne said, "How did you know, Amédée?"

Amédée shrugged. "I recognized him from Michelangelo's picture, that the schoolmistress showed us."

Grey hair receding from the noble forehead, grey beard stained as with tobacco, brown feet in sandals protruding from the *djellabah* hem. Both players sat on clouds like cushions floating in midair. "He was winning, but I could see that he was cheating. His opponent saw too, and laughed, and then they both laughed. Jehovah entreated the opponent not to take offence, calling him by name, and I learned that it was the devil Satanas."

"Aiee!" gasped Amédée's half-sister Angèle. She crossed herself, and several others followed suit.

"You hadn't noticed his horns?"

"That's just it. He didn't look like himself at all, or I'd have known immediately." A narrow face, some of it flaking off like dried mud off a car door. Sparse hair dyed coal black, showing grey at the roots. A goatee, possibly dyed too.

"You saw his feet?"

"He was wearing Wellington boots. They did have a hollow rattle when he shifted his legs. And he stank, at least one of them did. Like rancid sweat, like misery. Jehovah dealt another hand, and then I saw that they both were cheating."

"They spoke Galitois?" asked a half-brother.

"Jehovah like a native. The other fluently but with a thick accent, that sounded German."

"Uncle Amédée, were they playing for Grand-mother Rose's soul?"

"I don't think so. But they must have known she was about to expire."

Anne said, "Were you the prize then?"

"I hope not."

"What did you do, Papa?"

"What would you have done?"

Antoine thought. "You could have given the bad one his proper horns, by making the cuckold sign at him."

Marie-Rose spoke up. "If it were me, I'd have abased myself on the floor to the Jehovah. To show what a good child I can be."

"Shame on her," said a cousin two years Marie-Rose's senior, as if in an undertone to her neighbor, but in everyone's earshot. "She'd have wet her pants in fright, is what she'd have done."

Carmen smoothed back her daughter's hair. "But tell us, Cri-cri."

Amédée smiled. "I went down for a bottle of rosé and glasses, and a plate of *oreillettes*. Such illustrious visitors in my lighthouse, and it was all I could offer."

"What rosé, Amédée?" asked André, and Angèle exclaimed, "The *oreillettes* I sent you! Did you explain who baked them?"

Amédée spread his large hands on the figured linen kept for grave or joyous occasions. "The opportunity was denied me." He took a deep breath. "When I returned to the attic, they had departed. The light was still burning though, and. . . ." Lantern light swam in Amédée's dark lustrous eyes. ". . . I took that as a good omen." Grape leaves stirred once more above the assembled family, as though Rose were bidding them all adieu.

Before leaving La Galite, Amédée with his wife and children stopped by Conchette's bar and grocery to drink a toast to the fortune of the next three months. Conchette seldom stood drinks but this time she offered a round of champagne. She and Amédée having been occasional lovers in the past, people naturally accorded them a moment of tête-à-tête. By then, Conchette like the rest of the islanders had heard of Amédée's tale of supernatural visitation. ". . . if it had happened to me," she said, "I suppose I'd have been as quick to recount it."

Amédée said, "Come now, Conchette. You keep secrets better than anyone else on the island. A good thing too, for a bartender."

"What do you hear from Laurence?" Conchette asked. "Is she enjoying Sfax?"

Amédée thought of the conversation, and of Conchette's own reputed commerce with the supernatural, when he found an envelope from Laurence with the black stripe of condolence on his return to Tabarka. Laurence had heard of Rose's death, and wrote to send sympathy, and also to say that she had decided to move back up the coast to Bizerte, where she had found work cleaning hotel rooms, and where she and her daughter Thérèse would have the pleasure of seeing Anne and André and their sons from time to time. It went without saying that she would also be much closer to Tabarka. In his reply Amédée suggested that in three months' time, if he stopped overnight with Anne and André on his way to or from La Galite, it might be possible for him and Laurence to spend a few hours together, for the first time in, what? . . . he had to count, in four years already. He also wrote his customary brief note to Carmen and the children. The substitute keeper had nothing to report about his Tabarka week. Amédée settled into familiar routines of the barely discernible Tunisian winter, he forty-four, hale, and still with a certain beauty.

A week passed, a fortnight. Near noon, the middle of a day's sleep, Amédée woke with a start and saw that he was not alone in the dimness of his shuttered chamber. Counterclockwise around his bed capered a supernatural troupe, male and female, barefoot. They shook inaudible tambourines and threw back their heads in distant laughter, and scrutinized him with bright eyes when they passed near his face. Their rags and manner made them first seem wild as the black *abousadi* of Bizerte, of whom Amédée had heard frightening tales. He tried to sit up, found himself paralyzed and, near swooning from fear, understood that they were not human. So as not to waste the opportunity, he tried to say, "You must advise me," but managed only the first two words in a gurgle. One of the dancers, a female his age with loose inky hair, bent over him, rhinestones cascading from her earlobes. She laid a narrow hand over Amédée's mouth, whereupon sleep returned like a drug. Hours passed as in an instant, so that late in the afternoon Amédée woke with the unspoken "advise me" in his mind, and the room felt vacated.

That night out in the lighthouse Amédée tried to make sense of what had happened. A low tide coughed up sliding fragrances of iodine and rock.

The hand on his mouth could mean, be patient, he thought, advice will arrive in good time. Or yet—he listened to the shoreline susurrus—it could mean that his question was needless because—Amédée struggled for the proper construction—needless because what he already knew sufficed. If so, though, what might the visitation have betokened? Come morning, when the gears slowed to their timed halt, he would hear the ensuing silence. Now, for the past hour the quiet deep hum had sunk beneath his notice. Yet he could adjust his attention to hear it. With another adjustment, for the length of a heartbeat he could even almost hear it.

Amédée laid his cheek against his knuckles and considered other less heartening constructions of the visit, and even—a vertiginous swell crossed his mind —the possibility that it meant nothing. Was that possible? If so, might the same be true of—and now a familiar queasiness took him—true of love? Whereupon the still queasier possibility occurred to him that his vision had a significance he could never know, and so (poor Amédée!) with his entire life. Through the tissue beneath his left nostril, upper canine roots pressed against his left index finger knuckle. As he breathed, the pressure fluctuated, and with the tip of his tongue Amédée felt the tooth respond.

That tooth loosened further during the next nights and days. A week later it dropped out of Amédée's mouth, painlessly, and the same process had begun with several of its neighbors, lower as well as upper. Without informing Anne and her husband, so as not to alarm them, Amédée went to Bizerte to see the dentist of the Galitois, a Marseillais Amédée trusted for diagnosis and also for discretion. The man shook his head, sweeping a beam from his troubled forehead across Amédée's face. He could provide no explanation, and when he prescribed calcium supplements it was with little confidence. That night back in the Tabarka lighthouse Amédée took his weak chills to be a symptom of sleep debt, and the following day he gave himself two extra hours in bed. He slept well and yet as he woke he seemed to have suffered disquieting dreams, and the chills worsened that night in the light-house, so debilitating him that by morning he could barely pilot his bicycle across the causeway. He ate half a melon and some dried sardines, and fell straight to sleep.

Near noon he seemed to drift awake and only then realize with a sinking feeling that once again he had supernatural company, indeed the same troupe as before, less her who had touched his mouth. Not cavorting now, in fact scarcely moving, they ringed his bed and peered down at him like visitors about a coffin. As if from another world, outside Amédée heard a goat cross the square in the midday quiet, and tables being set. He waited, ready to die.

As if in response to his earlier unspoken request, the visitors now advised Amédée, that for two years he should abstain from carnal relations with Carmen, eat nothing from the sea, and give everything he earned to the poor, except for a modicum for his family. The visitors also told him that his teeth would continue to fall out until he had none. The chills would continue too, and would gradually usher him through death's door, unless he drank a decoction of asafoetida, oil of cloves, and purslane daily for a month, beginning as soon as possible. Amédée would have thanked them, were he not again alone in the dim room.

That evening before work he posted a letter to Anne asking her to bring him the three ingredients from Bizerte, without letting anyone besides André know of their destination. Five days later she arrived and found big Amédée weak as a baby. He hesitated to provide even her with an explanation, but Anne knew indirect ways to elicit confidences, and before he knew it he had apprised her of his visitations, and of the conditions laid down at the second. "Promise me you'll let no one know of these matters unless it be André."

Anne helped him raise his head to sip the potion. "They swore you to silence?"

Amédée swallowed. "If so, little Anne, do you suppose you could have plied me?" He frowned. "But it seems better, for all concerned, at least during my lifetime."

"I promise, in any case." Laving his brow, she smiled. "Not that it should cost me much. Who'd believe me? They'd call this a poor sequel after Jehovah and Satanas. But, Amédée: I was wondering what language they spoke."

Amédée sat up. "It must have been Galitois. I hadn't

thought because . . ." he pushed four large blunt fingers through dark silvering curls, "because I felt so little . . ." he searched for the word, "so little resistance."

Anne considered. Many details remained hazy—for instance, which poor? The question of Laurence crossed her mind too. Should Amédée break off his sporadic gifts of money to Laurence without explanation, it would be a hardship, and a wound to her spirit. Watching, Amédée divined something of Anne's thoughts, but he said nothing, and Anne contented herself with the suggestion that, before Carmen and the children should go hungry, she and André would deprive themselves.

Amédée followed the supernatural advice to the best of his ability and according to his lights. Replacing teeth was the first order of business. The imperturbable Marseillais fitted him according to order, omitting rear molars. An economy, the man supposed, and he was partly right, although he would never have imagined the destination for the saved money. Amédée furthermore wanted to honor qualms he felt about replacing any teeth. Carmen thought the changes in her husband's comportment all of a piece, and she hoped they might not prove permanent. Amédée's teeth wouldn't grow back, but his desire for her and for fish and crustaceans might return. Carmen was equally philosophic about his access of charity toward indigent mainland Galitois and Arabs. Her long-term planning went on hold but there was no need to cut week-to-week spending much. As for Laurence, Amédée continued her disbursements, telling himself that both authorized categories, the family and the poor, might subsume her. If the amount or frequency decreased, the change was too infinitesimal for her notice.

By the end of the two years Amédée's regime had grown so habitual that he was tempted to extend it for good measure, except that he didn't want to push his luck. Beggars in Tabarka and Bizerte wondered how they had offended him. Carmen knew that her husband's attentions to at least two other island women, far from falling off, had apparently increased. At length, with the help of one of those very women, old Conchette, Carmen had tried working a spell with chevrefeuille and a wishbone, which she supposed efficacious when his ardor returned.

4. CAUSES

In the next seventeen years the Galitois migrated off the island, south to newly independent Tunisia, and north to the coasts of France and Italy. Amédée and Carmen settled in Le Brusc on the French Mediterranean in a small house on a quieter street of the quiet village. Their children married and settled in Tunis (Antoine) and Naples (Marie-Rose). Anne and André and their sons settled in Toulon, and half a dozen siblings and friends also washed ashore onto the Côte d'Azur. As a minority within the minority of *pieds noirs* from North Africa, the Galitois of that littoral kept to themselves. At home they spoke Galitois, which their children understood without speaking, and which was a foreign language to grandchildren as they came along.

In France Amédée found lighthouse work on the island of Porquerolles, whose light was so securely automated and surveilled that the authorities chose not to replace him when he retired after five years in 1974. This island being inhabited, and near enough Le Brusc for semiweekly visits, Amédée's last stint of keeping had a humdrum character, nor did any untoward voice or vision enliven it. With the years, and especially in retirement, Amédée, never loquacious, settled more into his own ruminative silence, as he returned after more than thirty years to the ordinary pattern of nocturnal sleep and diurnal waking. The last memory many Galitois have of him is of a craggy grandfather folded like an ironing board in a corner, hands laced around a knee, and with a demeanor of the blind.

Amédée's death certificate, stamped and signed by the nephew of the circuit doctor, reads "The D'Arco house, La Galite, 5 October 1980, 0:00." The time and the precision of its notation may seem implausible, nor is that the only anomaly in the document, Carmen's copy of which, since her own death, now rests in the possession of Amédée's sister Anne, herself widowed a year before Carmen.

Carmen had been spared knowledge of Amédée's more troubling uncanny episodes until the heavy July morning in 1980 when she woke with the fear that he had died beside her. The sound of his breath reassured her and she turned to kiss him awake, but the sight of his face, swollen and discolored with bruises, so startled her that she cried out. As she told Anne later,

Amédée woke disoriented and it took her some effort to bring him to himself. He had been fighting for hours, in his sleep as he lay beside her and she slept peacefully—fighting for his life, he said, against beings intent on dismembering him. When Carmen helped him doff his burgundy silk pajamas, they found evidence of the struggle over his entire body, unlacerated but bruised and swollen. "Why? Have you done something wrong, Amédée?"

Amédée found his teeth on the night table and inserted them gingerly. "Probably I have." His voice was hoarse, and still feeble, and yet Carmen heard a familiar note of wistful teasing, that she knew to be affectionate. He continued, "It was not my intention, however."

"But when? Yesterday we. . . ."

Amédée waved a finger. "We were good yesterday. I watched our television. I read the newspaper." He seemed not to know what more to say. Then he said, "Don't fret. They shouldn't be back." Carmen couldn't tell whether he might say more. When he merely sighed she went to find an analgesic spray that relieved mosquito bites and couldn't be amiss, she thought, on the marks of Amédée's struggle, pain-

less though they were, and already subsiding. She returned and was misting his pale torso when he chose
to deliver himself of what else had been on his mind.
"I can't swear to it, but I believe they supposed I belonged to them. More than to you and the children—
or to any other earthly being, for that matter. They
came to take me piece by piece, little expecting such
resistance."

"They thought you theirs, Amédée?"

Amédée clicked his jaw sideways. "There's no accounting for tastes," he said.

That autumn, as the mistral blew down onto Provence, Amédée spoke of revisiting La Galite. The
Tunisian government honored property rights of the
scattered inhabitants, most of whom returned for a
week or two every few years. Amédée and Carmen
had last set foot on the island four years earlier, with
their two children, their daughter-in-law and a grandson. Now it was time, Amédée said, even though both
children had to beg off.

No one else happened to be on the island. The
jaunty sailor who dropped off the old couple had misgivings, and made them promise to radio the mainland daily during their stay. The Galiton lighthouse

having been automated by then, there were no fellow humans closer than Bizerte, forty kilometers to the southeast. On the second day Amédée told Carmen he wanted to pass a night alone in his old bedroom, up in Rose's house. Accustomed to his whims, and feeling more at home on La Galite than anywhere else, Carmen prepared an overnight bag for him and waved him off into the misty evening up the path past the bamboo grove, placid as when she had sent a child to spend a night with a friend. He was abstracted, she was to recall, and yet he showed an exceptional tenderness when he kissed her forehead.

"Did you dream, that you remember?" Anne asked. If she did, the morning's events erased every trace. The flutter and shush of a hydroplane coasting in to dock woke her. Like other islanders, Carmen associated the sound more with emergencies than with happy surprises. She dressed and hurried up to Rose's house, inclined to call out as soon as she was within earshot, yet holding silent as she crossed the bright peaceful clearing and the threshold, and the room for cooking and dining in bad weather, and the shadowy alcove giving onto the bedrooms. Here she slowed, to tidy her hair and also surely, she later realized, because she could hear someone approaching from the landing, and because she heard nothing else.

Like a welcome morning sunshine spilled through the doorway of the room Amédée and his brother and their half-brothers had slept in. On her skin Carmen could feel that Amédée had slept with windows open, as was his custom. She walked into the room.

On the bed near the window Amédée lay motionless in his silk pajamas. For an instant Carmen's eyesight seemed to have gone out of register, as could happen with the television set. Amédée's face and hands looked pale, while the sheet he lay on looked at once dark and flashing. "Cri-cri," she murmured, as if to reproach him ever so gently, for she now saw that he lay dead on the sheet darkened with blood, all his blood that had left his body and filmed the sheet, to dry and crack there, and leave his flesh a yellowed ivory.

Anne wondered whether his eyes were open or closed. Carmen had laid Amédée to rest not, as Anne suspected he would have preferred, on La Galite, but in the municipal cemetery of Le Brusc. November and December had passed, the holidays each widow had spent with children, January, and now Carmen had come to visit Anne at her house on a hillside above Toulon. The sisters-in-law drank weak coffee on Anne's sunny terrace. It was Anne's first chance to satisfy her curiosity about the circumstances of her brother's death.

His eyes nearly closed, Amédée had lain on his back on the bed of his youth, hands palm down at his sides. Smoothing closed his eyelids, Carmen noticed what she hoped and feared was a note to her on the bedside table, anchored with a stone. "Mr. and Mme. Conti?" Before responding, Carmen perused the leaf of paper and, seeing that it was not addressed to her, yet still guarding some hope for a last word, examined the dark surface about Amédée's right forefinger, in case he might have managed to make some mark there before it dried, but no. Then she walked back to the entrance, where the young doctor waited with an orderly and a stretcher.

The previous evening Amédée had radioed the doctor with a plausible description of symptoms of appendicitis, asking for his presence on the morrow. The ruse served primarily for Carmen's protection, for it brought almost immediate assistance, and allowed the doctor to certify the death with minimal delay. "I

waited at the grape arbor while they examined Amédée. It didn't take long. Anne, you should have seen
how the young doctor rose above himself. He told me
he knew no explanation. He couldn't even say how
Amédée's blood had left his body, or how it had dried
so quickly. Never mind why."

Anne listened. A late winter mistral had relented,
but the sunny air still had a chilly undertone. "I've
wondered about the blood myself, Carmen. I hope
you don't mind my asking whether it was buried with
the body."

Carmen nodded. "Most of it. Amédée had spread
one of Rose's oilcloth tablecloths under the sheet.
None of the blood had touched the mattress. I don't
understand how it could dry, even with the breeze.
Could some blood be more volatile than other?"

"I never heard of such a thing."

"Nor I, Anne. Anyhow, when they had Amédée on
the stretcher, they rolled up the sheet and oilcloth and
we took it away too. I had it laid in the coffin with him,
not unrolled, because the blood had mostly powdered
with the rolling." On the way down to the seaplane
some whispers of that dusky rose must have drifted
from the ends of the tube onto the stony path. "The

young doctor was good, though. He had come to the island in the past with his uncle, and he knew his way. His uncle must have spoken to him about us, because he was . . ." Carmen searched for the word.

"Respectful?" Anne suggested.

Carmen nodded. "He started when he read the page Amédée had left, but he didn't say a word. Then and there he signed and stamped it," the death certificate in Amédée's own hand. He must have found a model, for it follows the conventional form to the letter, except for the omission of a single word, the omission possibly noted by the attending physician and by Amédée's survivors, although none has mentioned it. Where the standard form reads ". . . of natural causes," Amédée's holograph simply reads, "of causes."

5. POST MORTEM

Anne's questions necessarily went unanswered at Amédée's funeral. Without himself being a believer, Amédée years earlier had let Carmen know that when the time came, should she choose a funeral for him, it would not constitute any betrayal of trust in his view.

In her view the service was due their children and the rest of the Galitois community. While most came from nearby to the chapel in Les Sablettes and the burial back at Le Brusc, Antoine and Marie-Rose and their families, and a few others, traveled from farther. Laurence sent condolences from Bizerte where her own precarious health kept her. Anne herself attended only the opening of the chapel service. It put her under such psychic strain—she having laid André to rest not thirteen months before—that she fainted and, upon recovering outside, chose not to disrupt the ceremony further by rejoining it.

Anne didn't bother to send Carmen a note of apology, for she well knew that her fainting had offered a tribute to Amédée's memory. Nor when Carmen came to drink weak coffee on Anne's terrace did the widows do more than routinely acknowledge the incident. Yet it had surprised and troubled her like a foretaste of her own mortality, and it set her to thinking, even during the television game shows she watched out of habit, and because André had enjoyed them. Shuffling from room to room in her empty house, Anne mulled over peculiarities of her life and those of those she loved and had loved, among them Amédée, whose photograph at the age of forty-odd she found in a plastic pocket of an album André had composed for her in the months when he must have felt his own time running out.

Amédée's face resisted Anne's scrutiny. He looked stolid rather than beautiful. Anne closed the album and retied its ribbon, and laid it into a fragrant drawer of the sideboard she and André had purchased two decades before. Nevertheless as time passed it seemed to Anne that she ought to revisit Tunisia.

At her age it wasn't easy. It seemed nearly impossible alone, and so she awaited a visit from her oldest son Yves, who had gone to live in America. Together they double-checked the closing of her house above Toulon, and a neighbor drove them down to the port for their embarkation on the ferry to Bizerte. The next morning they walked out on deck for a view of La Galite, but the ferry wasn't passing near enough. In Bizerte they stayed in an apartment around the corner from where Anne and André had lived when Yves and his brothers were children. Halfway through their three-week stay they hitched a trawler ride out to La Galite, with a picnic basket and sleeping bags.

Once they had left their things in the house Anne

had occupied with André, she and the son walked up to see Rose's house where she and Amédée were born and raised, and where he had died. Time seemed to have stood still here and indeed in all parts of the island they strolled to, including neglected gardens where long ago Amédée and Laurence had enchanted islanders with their duets of love. Grateful for Yves, a good son, and patient with an aging mother, Anne still couldn't help wishing she were strong enough to make this part of the voyage alone. It made her heart sink some to know that this good son, who had lived here himself, and who knew many of the old stories, even this child of her body, conceived in this very place forever ago, he with the best will in the world still could do no more than she to bridge the gulf between their respective apprehensions of the island and its history.

Before leaving Tunisia they visited Laurence where she lived in a suburb of Bizerte, on the fifth floor of a building that smelled like a hospital even though Yves assured Anne that it was rather what he called a rest home. Laurence had lived there a good four years, since her eyes had made it impossible to keep the apartment two doors from Anne and André's old address, where she had lived with her daughter Thérèse for seven years, and then alone for twenty-one more after her life had come to a halt, as the Galitois put it, because of Thérèse's accidental death in the shower caused by a water heater gas leak. Laurence hastened to explain that she could distinguish her visitors through her alarmingly protuberant clouded eyes. The son said next to nothing during the afternoon. His armchair near the window creaked now and then as he, a white and grey blob whose head expanded and contracted, leaned forward or away. Tiny Anne, having shrunk with the years, perched nearer Laurence's daybed, on the corner of the divan, and helped pour syrupy mint tea.

The women, utterly at ease with one another, and glad of what both knew would likely prove their last meeting, took their time to handle subjects of moment. Yet they conversed efficiently, and had covered much ground by the time Anne and Yves, and Laurence, bade one another goodbye.

When the talk turned to Amédée, it was the mid-afternoon hour of the *assr* and the muezzin's chant broadcast from the city center, summoning the faithful to prayer, drifted in through palm fronds. After a moment Anne asked, easily as if it were inevitable, whether Amédée had ever spoken to Laurence about his voices.

"More times than I can count. I took it as a confidence, while he was alive. We wondered if I might hear them. I put my ear against his when he was hearing one, just touching. His ear was cold—I suppose all ears are—and big even then, so that the lobe tickled my neck, but I listened for all I was worth. We both listened, but only Amédée heard. Later, once after we had been together here in Bizerte—this young man would have been an infant—Amédée had done his week out on La Galite and was returning to Tabarka, one of the times he stopped with you and André, remember? About this time of day Amédée seemed to doze and then he said I should put my ear against his like in the old times, if I wanted to hear a chuckling voice. I did as he said. Nothing, as before, but this time I couldn't be sure he wasn't playing a game."

Anne said, "After we grew up, we didn't speak of those voices he had once been so proud of. I've wondered since, did they too speak Galitois, like his unearthly visitors?"

"Unearthly," Laurence breathed. "Yes, they talked Galitois. I didn't ask, but Amédée sometimes found relief by confiding things in me he didn't share with Carmen. His voices might sing a few words in a language strange to him, or merely make sounds, like water talking to itself. When they did talk, they said only a word or two, like riddles. He could never be sure whether they were male or female, or old or young. Almost always he knew they were mocking him, and sometimes they laughed. A few times though he heard a whole sentence from the beyond. When that happened, he thought he also heard pity."

After a moment Laurence continued, "Amédée never quoted me any such message. He said they weren't worth it, and another time he suggested that they were cryptic or nonsensical. But once or twice Amédée said something that sounded as if he might be citing one of those messages. Once after midnight we left Thérèse sleeping and walked by the Bizerte harbor, in a rising wind that made the boat lines sing. I said it was unearthly. After a moment Amédée agreed. Then he sighed and shook his head, and he said, earthly too, it's the same in the end."

Anne nodded, thought, and nodded again, more decisively. "He came to love Carmen, but I doubt that he ever took a midnight stroll with her." She turned to her son. "Amédée and Laurence loved each other before you were born."

Laurence said, "Thérèse called him Uncle. She loved him. She may have wondered whether he was her father. He wasn't but . . ." she searched for the right phrasing, "but he might have been." The same question crossed three minds: in that case, might Thérèse now be alive?

Anne poured second cups. She told Yves, "Amédée never stopped being in love with Laurence. I think he always wished she could have been his wife."

Laurence sipped the infusion. She licked her lips, and then proceeded to tell her visitors the true story, that Amédée had rejected her rather than vice versa. "No one else knows, and I expected to take the secret with me to my own grave, but what can it matter now? I know I can count on your discretion, Anne, and I trust this young man too. In any case, away in America who could he tell?"

Anne shook her head. "But Laurence, can you guess why?"

Laurence nodded. "I know why. Furthermore I will tell you, since you've done me the kindness of visiting me here, and also because . . . because it seems a restitution. I'll tell you and this handsome son you're lucky to have. He has André's hair and eyes, no? The rest you, and maybe a touch of Amédée's jaw? I'll tell you both what I've never told anyone, not even Amédée, much as I would have liked to. Had I known at the moment of rupture, I suspect I would have told him. But I didn't learn why Amédée had rejected me until years later. We were both married by then. He had his children and I had Thérèse."

"Wait. You mean Amédée himself didn't know why he broke off with you?"

Creak, creak—the same question seemed to be exercising the blurred young American. Laurence shrugged. "Think, Anne. Haven't you ever done something without knowing why?"

Anne sniffed. "Of course. But never anything so consequential, for heaven's sake."

"Maybe," said Laurence with a trace of a smile. "But it happened this time. Amédée didn't know why he was doing what he did, and he knew he didn't know. At least he knew that much."

Anne set down her glass and spread her graceful arthritic hands in the air. "What are you saying, Laurence?" She gave a constricted exhalation that meant, "Don't make me laugh."

Chin in the heel of her hand, a fingertip beneath

each eye, as if to keep the globes in place, Laurence savored the moment, she who once had been beautiful, and had sung dark lullabies for her daughter, nursery and childhood songs, and later songs. Anne savored the moment too, and so within the limits of his capacity did her son. Laurence swirled her tea. Instead of drinking, she clinked down the glass. "Conchette made him do it."

"Conchette? But . . ." Anne interrupted herself to remind Yves of Conchette's bar and grocery. "Conchette died in the mid-eighties. She's buried on La Galite. She had truck with the supernatural, to be sure, and she could have changed Amédée's mind with one of her charms." She turned to Laurence. "Except, even when you and he were melting every heart, even then didn't he and Conchette sometimes. . . ."

"Even before. Conchette was his first woman, if I'm not mistaken."

"Excuse me." The long head expanded out of the haze in the wing chair. "Wasn't Conchette quite a bit older than Amédée?" Certainly in the son's memory, the squat grocer more of Rose's generation than Amédée's.

A glance between Laurence and Anne. Anne patted

what seemed her son's knee. "The Galitois didn't much worry about such things."

Laurence said, "Amédée especially not. But, no, there was no jealousy on Conchette's part, I don't think, or possessiveness. She'd been widowed a decade then. She must have been glad of the attentions of a handsome boy, but there were another two or three young men for whom she served as . . . tutor."

"And some not so young," interjected Anne. "So why should she care if you and Amédée lived together happily ever after?"

"She wouldn't have cared a fig, I think. My father was the one that cared. Conchette told me, after his death. It was at his request that she put a spell on Amédée and made him marry Carmen." Laurence blinked. "But not even Conchette could stop Amédée from loving me."

"No," mused Anne. "Conchette couldn't reach into hearts. But did she owe your father something, do you suppose, to do him that service?"

"Who knows. Papa may have remunerated her, or possibly he had otherwise succored her some time or other. She must have had her reasons though."

"And, knowing her, she took them with her." Anne

paused and then said, "Our two fathers were childhood friends, no? And later too. I barely remember
Eugène, but I do remember hearing that your father
knew him better than anybody else on the island. Isn't
it curious then for him not to want Eugène's son as a
son-in-law?"

Knock, knock. Without awaiting an invitation, a
nurse stuck her head in to say that the hour for Laurence's procedures was approaching. Anne and Yves
took the cue to rustle and rise and begin their extended leave-taking, with kisses and vows, and a few
more reminiscences and revelations, including this
from Laurence as she held Anne's hands in one of hers
and patted them with the other. "As I was about to
say a moment ago—I'm not batty yet, you see—I can
tell you a touch more about why Papa went to such
lengths to keep me and Amédée apart. Papa alluded to
it only once, and with a troubled sadness. He seemed
to fear that Eugène Conti's death might not have been
caused by a Moroccan fever after all."

Anne frowned. "He thought Maman's royal noti-
fication false? I've kept it for Yves and his brothers."

"He didn't suspect the Moroccan government of in-
tentional untruth, Anne. Anyhow it was only a rumor,

that had filtered back into Algeria, that Papa heard over there in some port. Papa doubted that Rose ever heard the story, not any other Galitois for that matter. What came over Eugène did so in less than a week, and the foreman of his road crew did choose to call it a fever, but apparently during that time all the other men felt Eugène being pulled away from them. He died in pain and fear, Papa heard, and in a shameful and not quite involuntary manner. Abashed by what they had witnessed, the crew disbanded and went their separate ways.

"Papa may well have kept some details about this from me, and in my turn I thought it best not to burden Amédée or you then with such uncertain information. But Papa did seem to fear that Amédée might have inherited a . . . a susceptibility of Eugène's, that would grieve me if we married.

"But enough. Goodbye, Anne, goodbye, young man. If you can believe, they'll have me processed and fed and watered before nightfall, before *maghreb*, so that they can be home for dinner. Goodbye, goodbye. How I wish Amédée. . . ."

At their deserted bus stop shelter on the silent avenue, Yves asked Anne if she and Laurence had been girlhood friends. Not exactly—Anne hadn't been one to socialize, Laurence either, come to think of it, and she then had been too preoccupied with Amédée. The tall young man, like his brothers a good son, and handsome despite his foreign haircut and thinness, and the small old woman who shrank microscopically if you took your eyes off her for even a second, and who by all rights might be submitting to the wear of the afternoon, yet already had the next meal planned, waited side by side on the gridded translucent plastic bench, with scarcely a thought of how grateful Amédée would be for them, and for the lingering light.

TOUCH WOOD

▼

A forty-three-year-old long-divorced Cincinnati dental hygienist sits alone at a table in the deserted plaza of a village in northern Spain, late summer evening three or four years ago, where she has come for the single free day of the two-week three-country group tour her prosperous brother offered her for a birthday present. The purple shadow of the clock tower lengthens across the paving stones. In one of the dusty plane trees a cicada whines. The woman sips a heavy liqueur that holds in suspension flakes of actual gold.

The woman has no hope of seeing sidle from the taverna the young Moroccan who touched her two years ago with a poisonous mixture of protectiveness and desire, when he sidled into the minty suburban Cincinnati office with a toothache and a doubtful chit for payment. He is probably in Morocco now, cobbling together a living while he angles for the heart of yet another American, one willing to grant him citizenship by marriage, he hopes—and how much is it to ask, after all, any more?

But this village square with its dribbling fountain and mountains just visible resembles, she imagines, his childhood one in Morocco, and furthermore the names are similar. Yet even should he materialize here with his slight limp, what difference would it make? The woman has no regrets about the clean break she effected more than ten months ago. Now is the time for taking account and charting a course. The Madrid bus should rattle back into the plaza near eight.

The woman studies her ticket. Letters and numerals lie inert on the paper and yet there glimmers—and in her own language yet, if numerals were letters—an invitation. "Look up." The woman listens. She hears a distant cowbell, and now a near footfall. She looks up, to see a beggar approaching—at least she supposes him one of that pestering tribe, until at her table he mumbles something, perhaps to her, before continuing across the dead square into a blue vista. The woman's Spanish permits her to understand his words to have been, "Telephone him immediately."

"How silly," thinks the woman. As if she could find a Tangier number, if he were there and with a phone. As if there could be any point in resuming negotiations when, in any case, the bus is due already and missing it would mean sleeping here, and losing half a day of the tour. The woman shrugs and drops pesetas into the dish. She hears the bus, and stands and crosses to meet it, with the merest flicker of amusement at her momentary susceptibility to an inexplicable prompting.

In Tangier the woman's ex-lover is constructing the message he will soon leave on her Cincinnati recorder, and which she will never hear. He has attained dual US-Moroccan citizenship and plans to return to Cincinnati. More than ever, he loves and desires the woman. While marriage would still please him best, any other arrangement to her liking would also please him and, out of gratitude and love, even should she wish never to see him again, he hopes she will allow him to bestow on her a large part of the staggering fortune he has just inherited.

The message does not reach the woman because the bus returning her to Madrid throws a rod and she, the lone passenger, pacing in the dusk, loses her footing and, tumbling down an escarpment, breaks both wrists and, worse, scrapes a forearm where she develops a galloping infection that two days later in Seville proves fatal.

Some have profited from this story. A young man hearkened, despite reservations grown all but instinctive. Before he finished reading he felt the story changing his life. Not that everything changed utterly, but the small decisive change went deep, the man knew. He looked at his thumb on the paper, its nail and its shadow. He recalled a morning in his childhood when, reading on a sofa, he had felt the world reconstituting itself around him after an indeterminate absence. As on that distant morning, much now shifted in the flicker of an eye. Without asking how or why this story had repeated the effect, the man thanked his lucky stars.

The next day, when he had occasion to think of the story, he thought well of it—not perhaps as well as he knew it deserved, and yet very well, and he spoke similarly of it. That afternoon it rained, a long hush. Listening, the man recognized the power and excellence of this story as his own, and he quickly made two seemingly difficult choices. By week's end both had proved correct. Today this man enjoys professional success beyond his years, and perfect health and lasting love.

On the other hand, a man three days shy of sixty, at the apogee of a distinguished career, had the misfortune to dismiss this same story, which he had read by chance and with growing impatience, filling an hour among other browsers and searchers in a university reading room with high windows and busts. He dismissed and later denigrated this story. The delayed consequences included the gravest public exposure of misconduct the man had hardly admitted to himself. That man now lives in disgrace and ridicule with a contemptuous companion in the country. They move often and find it ever more difficult to make ends meet.

A short blonde Minnesota lesbian, aged twenty-three, took this story to heart. She pressed her copy on her cousin and his wife, dry cleaners in their mid-thirties, who also found themselves moved and touched. Indeed all three found themselves entering into this story. Troy Duckworth, the lesbian, discovered an unsuspected gift for sexing corn tassels, which she patented and which, in a roundabout fashion, figured in her subsequent development of the cure for an hemorrhagic tropical virus. Henry and Helen Mimmer, the dry cleaners, have expanded into Wisconsin.

In contrast, a retired television executive sniffed when she sampled this story (which she had no business reading in the first place), and she mentioned it slightingly to a friend and her chauffeur. Six weeks later the rash woman's niece gave birth to a child with a club foot. Other instances could be cited, with the most widely varying rewards and punishments. A deadness might settle over everything including television news, and the victim never notice the change. It is difficult to imagine.

Jay, a white single middle-aged American urban pioneer in a lawless tropical city, steps off the last verandah of the developed quarter. He passes scrub palmettos in still moonlight, crosses a long-covered swimming pool, and mounts a tangled ridge. According to the real estate agent, access to the ocean may be had this way, the most direct route if the least perspicuous, leading Jay through a brown and black slum.

Atop the ridge, from shadows steps an ashen black warlord accompanied by darker thugs. Without so much as a by-your-leave, the man clips the shoulder strap of Jay's point-and-shoot and tosses the toy to a factor. As negligently he relieves Jay of his wallet and pocket change. Not yet visible, the ocean casts its spell from beyond what must be a last ruined hillock of alleys and derelict hotels.

Behind tinted steel-rimmed glasses, the warlord's humorless eyes survey Jay, who can feel debris beneath the soles of his sandals. Bad luck it would certainly be to die at the man's whim, flayed or the throat slit.

The man shrugs at Jay and his fortunes, his pleated trousers. With his chin the man indicates the route to the beach, and yet he counsels Jay to turn back. Once, he says, Jay's kind might have been tolerated, but it's too late to reverse the clock now. Be reasonable. Not even gringos have better than one life. Return where you belong unless you fancy ending as a caged philosopher, like him under that sewer grate—those his wispy fingers—speculating day and night for all he's worth. He supposedly could read Greek, were any available.

Into their nocturnal agenda fade the capo and his henchmen, and Jay proceeds up the tangled hill in the gathering darkness and wind. Up the stair of a narrow abandoned building, through a door ajar, Jay finds a dry room with a light burning. Probably he can stay here until morning unnoticed by marauders.

He ignores the Bombay gin left conveniently on the table, and considers the future. Will he live with pigeons on park benches? Will he beg? Jay eases himself to the floor and lies there. In the weak steady light he hears a rustle like surf, and a pinging. Deep perplexity gathers to a wave. Good comes of it.